The Best Man

By

Adriana Kraft

The Best Man
By
Adriana Kraft

ISBN: 978-0-9894693-3-3

B&B Publishing
1970 N. Leslie St. #560
Pahrump, NV 89060

Cover by
Dawné Dominique
DusktilDawn Designs

CHAPTER ONE

Groaning politely, Kitty Paige stared at the ceiling of the hotel suite trying to encourage the young man between her legs, who was doing his best to satisfy her. He had a ways to go.

His tongue had felt like sandpaper when he'd made what was apparently the obligatory pass at pleasuring her orally. At least he did have some staying power. He'd been pounding his cock in and out of her for the past five minutes. Finesse was not her daughter's groom's best man's strong suit — selecting him was clearly not her best cougar moment.

She scowled at the plaster ceiling swirls. She thought his name was Jason something or other.

Perhaps it was a mistake to have him join her to finish that last bottle of champagne. Each of the four young men standing up with Brad was a hunk, just like her soon to be son-in-law, but the best man had caught her eye more than the others. He carried himself proudly and appeared very agile. She'd thought he had considerable promise for one night.

She didn't expect to hang around Seattle longer than that. The weather was too damn dreary. As soon as her daughter and new husband were on

1

their way to Puerto Vallarta for their honeymoon, she'd be heading back to Chicago — she could get a decent cup of coffee there, too.

She glanced down at the back of the young man's head resting on her breastplate. He seemed quite taken with watching himself glide in and out of her. Or maybe he was trying to remember what was supposed to happen next. She exhaled. Enough was enough.

"I'm ready, Jason." She hoped she had his name right. If not, he didn't try to correct her. She tapped his butt with her heels. He had to be ready. If she hadn't pinched his cock earlier, he would've come in her mouth when she'd gotten him wet before tugging the condom on his shaft. "Come in me, boy."

He lifted his head and nodded. "Yes, ma'am." He rose onto his hands and knees, altering his angle of penetration, and renewed his thrusting.

She tilted her pelvis slightly and slid a hand down between them to caress her clitoris. She wasn't going to be left out of this little crescendo. *He* might not know how to bring her off, but *she* did.

"Damn, you're hot," he grunted, watching her claw at her clit.

She grinned around clenched teeth when she felt his cock expand. He made no sound. She could only hear the slap of his hips against hers.

Her eyes popped wide open when he abruptly pulled out of her.

"I came," he announced. He glanced at her fingers still working on her clit. "Wasn't it good for you?"

Ah, hell. She withdrew her hand. She'd take care of it later. "Sure," she said. "You're quite the stud. Now I need to get my beauty sleep to be rested for Susan and Brad's wedding. I hope you don't mind, but I rest best sleeping alone."

"No problem," the young man said, sitting up. "I'd better get out of here or we might be at each other all night."

"That might be delightful, but it would be taxing. You run along and I'll see you tomorrow."

She watched himchap carefully dress. After he buckled his belt and buttoned the last button on his shirt, he gave her a crooked smile. "I won't forget this night, Mrs. Paige. You were fantastic." He winked at her. "Hotter than your daughter."

Kitty jerked straight up. "Hotter than…" She covered her mouth and swallowed. "You fucked Susan."

He frowned. "Of course. No big deal. All the guys standing up have had her at least once. Doubt there'll be many guys attending the wedding who haven't. Now she's Brad's exclusively. Oh well."

Kitty tilted her head to the side. She couldn't think of a thing to say. He waved at her as he headed for the door. "Bye. Susan's hot, but you're hotter."

When the door shut behind her most recent

lover, Kitty slid down under the covers. She wanted to hide. She wanted to be back in Chicago, in her own home in the north suburbs. Jesus, she'd just fucked one of her daughter's former lovers.

How did that make her feel? Creepy, but then he'd made her feel creepy even before making his little comparative announcement. Old. Damn. Was she that old? Of course she was. Her daughter was twenty-two. She'd had her when she was nearly eighteen. She'd put too much faith in a condom and too much faith in the high school quarterback. Damn, that added up to forty—but she wasn't forty yet. She had a little while left before crossing that threshold.

She'd loved Susan with all her heart and soul. She'd done her best to raise her well, and Susan had done well for herself. She'd graduated with honors from Loyola with a degree in psychology. Apparently, she'd also earned kudos for bedroom skills.

Kitty inhaled sharply. She could hardly chastise her daughter for honing those skills. Before Susan had moved into the college dorms, Kitty had tried to be fairly discreet with her own lovers. It wasn't that she wanted to hide them from Susan, but she'd chosen not to flaunt them, either.

The girl had asked for permission to go on the pill after her sixteenth birthday party. Susan had given her the *just in case I do* argument. Kitty had consented. While Susan was the best thing that ever happened to her, she didn't wish premature

4

motherhood on her daughter.

Kitty peered at the door to the suite and let out a deep sigh. That was it. She'd fucked the best man, and he'd fucked Susan. She couldn't take that back. He'd only given her a lot of consternation. And she hadn't even come.

Kitty rolled over and hugged a pillow. She'd get through tomorrow. She'd gotten through a lot over the years. But how could she look at the men at her daughter's wedding without wondering which ones had slept with the bride?

- o -

Leaning against the banquet room wall, Jared Jacobs surreptitiously studied his prey one more time. The tall shapely blonde in the canary yellow dress and yellow stilettos had drawn his attention from the moment he'd seen her walking her daughter down the aisle.

She'd escorted the bride with her chin up and with a satisfied smile on her ruby lips. Apparently she and her daughter didn't mind thumbing their noses at custom. Unlike many mothers of the bride he'd seen, this one did not carry a Kleenex in her hand. She probably didn't have any in her tiny clutch purse, either. Tears wouldn't come naturally to the fair-skinned female exuding confidence at the chapel and here at the reception.

She appeared to laugh easily enough with acquaintances at the table where she was seated.

But a careful observer would note that her laughter seldom reached her eyes. Like him, she was a sharp observer. She'd assessed everyone in the room, particularly the men. When her gaze had settled on his from across the room, she'd lingered ever so briefly before moving her attention to the person standing next to him.

The small band began to play in earnest. Considerable banter and movement was occurring at the head table, where the groom helped his bride to her feet. Jared smiled. The traditional first dance was about to begin.

He glanced back at the woman in yellow. Why hadn't she sat at the head table along with the wedding party and the groom's parents? He liked a woman who did things her way — to a point. He welcomed a challenge of most any kind. He had little doubt the woman in yellow would be a challenge.

No one had bothered to introduce him to the mother of the bride. He'd made a point to find out what he could about her. Kitty Paige lived in Chicago. Never married, she'd raised her daughter by herself. To her credit, Susan had done well in school, in her profession and now in marriage. Her mother had little formal education beyond high school and apparently had no need for a husband. She certainly had no need for a husband's second income. According to his sources, Kitty Paige was acknowledged, grudgingly by some, as one of the top ten most successful realtors in the Chicago area, specializing in high end residential and commercial properties. She could likely buy and sell anyone in the room.

He smiled to himself. Well, most anyone. Jared combed his narrow mustache with his fingers and pushed away from the wall. The dance floor was already getting crowded.

- o -

Kitty lifted her chin as soon as the broad shouldered mustached man headed in her direction. She knew what he wanted. He'd been studying her much of the afternoon and evening. She was surprised it took him this long to come after her.

She offered him a thin smile. How many times had he undressed her in his mind? Maybe as often as she'd undressed him. He was easy to look at. Probably late forties, early fifties at most. Fit. No pot belly, which she despised. Graying around the temples. Square chin and a cute mustache. Kitty shivered slightly, imagining how that Clark Gable mustache would feel rubbing against sensitive spots.

She checked her watch and grimaced. Too bad she was catching the redeye back to Chicago — there wouldn't be time to satisfy her mustache curiosity.

"May I have this dance, Ms. Paige?"

Trying to look appropriately surprised, Kitty peered into dark brown eyes that sparkled. He clearly knew she wasn't surprised.

"Of course," she said, rising to her feet.

She let him guide her to the small dance floor. She moved into his arms, trying not to react to his warm smile. He was accustomed to holding a woman. He held her close comfortably, resting a hand on the rise of her rump. "I'm afraid you have me at a disadvantage," she said, eyeing him levelly. "You know my name, but I don't know yours."

"Jared Jacobs."

"Friend of the groom, or the bride? I'm afraid since Susan moved out here, I don't know most of her friends."

"I've been a friend of Brad's family for years. I've met Susan several times. You've done a fine job raising your daughter, Ms. Paige."

"Thank you. Do call me Kitty. Ms. Paige makes me sound too motherly. So do you live in Seattle?"

"Nope. I'm a fan of the sun. I work out of San Diego."

"That should be sunny enough. You say *work out of*. Don't you live there, too?"

"You're not only a beautiful woman and a lovely dancer, you're a good listener."

The music stopped for more toasts by the best man.

"And you're a bullshit artist." She laughed at his scowl. "I'm not easily charmed—unless I want to be. So you haven't answered my question."

"I'm a businessman. I have several interests," Jared said, handing her a glass of champagne. "I'm a middle man for various overseas companies seeking buyers in this country — copper, steel, aluminum. Most anything, really."

"So you travel a lot."

"Maybe that's why it feels like I work out of San Diego rather than live there. I understand you're a successful business woman yourself."

She shrugged her shoulders. "That's a matter of opinion. There's always room for improvement."

"I also travel some to follow my horses."

"Horses?"

"Race horses. Do you ever get out to Arlington Park?"

"Of course. It's such a beautiful place." She'd heard the catch in his voice when he mentioned the horses. She understood the awe those majestic animals could inspire. "I've been to the Derby a couple times."

"Ah, so you have more than passing interests in the addictive beasts." He gave her a broad smile, took her hand and guided her back to the dance floor.

"Doesn't every girl dream about horses?"

"Most girls give up their childhood fantasies as reality smacks them in the faces." He leaned away from her as they swayed to the music. "Somehow, I don't think you do."

She grinned. "Maybe I should've, but I'm too

stubborn for my own good. Someday I'm going to own a racehorse. I just haven't gotten around to it yet."

"Maybe you haven't found the right partner?"

She saw his eyes teasing before she rested her head on his shoulder. "Maybe I've been too busy to look." She'd add racehorses to her *to do* list as soon as she got back to Chicago. She had plenty of contacts. She might not have given up on her childhood fantasy, but she'd nearly forgotten it. She smiled into Jared's suit coat. Maybe her daughter's wedding would rekindle a dream.

They danced to the slow music. Kitty smiled at the other couples on the floor. Most were rooted in place. Jared apparently liked to dance. They moved easily together.

They danced in silence. By the third song in the set, they were in a darkened corner moving no more than anyone else. His large hands curved around her butt. She'd laced her fingers behind his neck.

"Um," he whispered. "You smell heavenly."

Kitty hid her smile. She'd been thinking the same thing about him. She couldn't determine if it was his cologne or his manliness. "If you think you're dancing with an angel, you're going to be disappointed."

His fingers dug into her bottom. She wanted to purr when she felt his arousal growing larger. She'd been aware of its presence for a while, but now it was rising to serious proportions. Too bad she had a plane to catch.

She swayed on her tiptoes, grinding her pubic bone against his thickening penis. If the ballroom had been darker, she would've lifted a leg to cradle his butt.

"Jesus," Jared said, gasping into her ear. "Jackson said you were hot."

Kitty jerked out of his grasp. "What?" She narrowed her eyes and ground her fists against her waist. "What the hell did you say?"

"Don't make a scene," he said, in a low breath grabbing her hand. "Remember your daughter."

Heeding his advice, she let him hurry her out an exit to the hallway, where she whirled on him. "Explain yourself, you bastard. Who the hell is Jackson?"

"I'm sorry," Jared said, turning redder still. "The words just came out. I hadn't expected you to try to get yourself off that way."

"I wasn't." Her denial didn't ring true, even to her ears. She'd lost her bearings there for a moment. She never lost her bearings, particularly with a man. "What the hell did you mean?" She had him on the defensive, and that was where she wanted to keep him.

"Jackson. Jackson Jacobs. My son. The best man."

"The best man," she gagged. "Your son. Hot! You bastard."

"But that didn't have anything to do with me wanting…"

"A piece of the bride's mother? Dream on." Kitty gave him her best icy glare—the one she'd practiced as a young woman before her bedroom mirror. No man could withstand it. "I hope for the sake of any woman you ever hook up with, you're a hell of a lot better than your son." She peered down her nose. "But that seems doubtful. Thank God I've got to catch a plane."

She spun on her heel and marched down the hallway, leaving him fumbling for words.

- o -

Struggling for breath and equilibrium, Jared watched the shapely ass covered in yellow satin strut away from him. It was tempting to chase after her, press her against the wall, and convince her why she shouldn't be worrying about making a plane.

"She is hot," he growled, jamming a fist against the carpeted wall. Damn, how had those words slipped out of his mouth? He never fucked up like that, not with a woman.

Shit. They'd been so close. He could swear he'd felt her juices pooling as she'd begun to rub her pussy against his stiff cock in earnest.

He looked down the empty hall. Maybe she had more self-discipline than he did. He tugged on the corner of his mustache. Closing his eyes, he easily recalled every curve of the woman in yellow.

He smiled. She must like yellow. Would she

like yellow roses? He didn't take having a woman rebuff him easily, even if it was his mistake that led her to explode.

Kitty Paige might be a bigger challenge than he'd expected, but he was sure she'd also make a very worthy conquest. It might be fun to get to know her better. A woman of complexity intrigued him.

And she was that. A successful business woman. An able mother. A woman comfortable enough in her own skin to flaunt her beauty. She dressed hot, talked hot and apparently fucked hot. She should know better than to compare a youngster, even his son, with a mature man. Jackson probably had no clue what he'd held in his arms.

But *he* did. Not entirely, though. She wrapped her persona in enough mystery that it would take some time to really know her. Yet he knew a few things about her. She had a fascination for yellow, a fascination for race horses, and—at least briefly—a fascination for his cock.

That was enough to move forward on. He turned and whistled softly, making his way down the hall toward his hotel room. He'd have to call his trainer. Surely they must have a horse or two in their string they could ship to Arlington Park.

- o -

Lifting a leg above the steamy, sudsy water,

13

Kitty washed it carefully. She paid it the same sort of attention she'd devoted to her other leg, her arms, her breasts and her loins. There wasn't much she enjoyed more than a thorough soak and scrubbing. Like lovemaking, she believed a bath should seldom be rushed.

She'd realized long ago that for her, bathing was an act of self-love. She had no qualms about that. There was long period in her life when she hadn't had the time for such pleasure.

Kitty tucked her leg back under the hot water and rested her head on the lip of the tub. This was a luxury she'd earned. Never again would she work for a boss—male or female. She thoroughly enjoyed being her own boss. Any mistakes she made were hers. The same could be said for her successes.

She closed her eyes, replaying her trip to Seattle. Although never pleased with redeye flights, she felt like a soothsayer having booked that return trip. Events swirled too rapidly in the Pacific Northwest, even for her.

She sighed and yawned. No matter what people said about traveling first class, the seating space was still too confined to get a good rest. Though she had to admit that was better than traveling in coach with the other sardines.

She hoped Susan would be as happy in the future as she looked on her wedding day. Some of Kitty's divorced friends rued the day of their marriages. Everything apparently went downhill from there.

Kitty scrunched her shoulders together. She peered through eyelashes at her breasts breaking the surface of the water. Her nipples immediately pebbled under the cooler air temperature, causing her to smile. She wouldn't know about weddings. She'd never had one. And that was fine with her.

She'd never had to worry whether a husband remained faithful to her. And — she searched and found the bar of soap under the water — she didn't have to wonder if she could be faithful. Remaining single meant she could pretty much find a cock whenever she needed one without all the domestic expectations and inevitable grief.

She had no need to depend upon a man, and more importantly, no need to trust one. She only had to rely on her good sense and judgment.

She winced — she hadn't used such good sense after the rehearsal dinner. Uncharacteristically, she'd been whipping herself over that one all the way back from Seattle. Usually she let misadventures roll off her back, trying to learn from them and move one.

This one still gnawed at her gut. What the hell was the best man's name? His dad had called him Jackson, right? It didn't really matter. Her vibrators were a hell of a lot more reliable than his cock. She smirked and pushed the soap bar down to her pubic area. She shouldn't blame his cock. It was rather nicely proportioned, actually. Too bad its owner didn't know how to use it to its fullest

15

potential.

She'd had decent young lovers before, but Jackson wasn't among their ranks. Still, she preferred an older man who knew how to treat a woman like she was aging wine. She preferred long sensuous lovemaking—she slid the soap bar down one side of her labia and back up the other—like a luxurious bath. She wasn't opposed to primal fucking, either; she could do quick and hard, but that had to be with a man who knew what he was doing. She wasn't going to be any guy's fuck doll to simply be used to bring himself off—quickly or not—without paying attention to her needs, too.

She spread her labia between the fingers of one hand and eased the soap along the resulting crevice. The damn kid hadn't even helped her come.

The image of the thin mustached father crept into her awareness. His smile disarmed her, making her shiver. "Damn," Kitty moaned, widening her thighs. The soap bar slid farther in. She slid it back and forth, cleansing her inner reaches and gulping for air. He'd been right. She'd been close to climaxing as she ground her pubic bone against his massive cock. Clothes weren't going to prevent her from that pleasure, but his words had certainly jolted her out of any pre-orgasmic haze.

Her fingers stilled below the water's surface. How much had his son told him about her? She grazed her navel. Did Jared know she wore a belly ring? She eased the soap bar in and out of her vulva again. Did he know she kept her pussy bare of all pubic hair? He wouldn't have to be bothered with getting little hairs caught in his teeth.

Kitty trailed fingers from her belly ring to her clit. She stroked it between thumb and forefinger, keeping time with the soap cleansing her pussy. What would his tiny mustache feel like pressed against her pussy lips? Would it tickle? Would it scratch? And if it did, would he soothe her with his tongue?

"Good God," Kitty panted, leaning forward and jerking against her fingers and the soap bar. Her head bobbed up and down as she sought release, as she welcomed release.

At last she sighed and settled back into the warm water. It had been a long time building — since before the wedding. What a strange little trip she'd taken.

She shuddered once again, imagining Jared's dark head between her legs sipping at her flow. Instead, her juices merely mingled with the bathwater. She smiled. That seemed like a waste, even to her.

Once she'd gotten out of the tub and dried herself with a large Turkish towel, Kitty sat down at her makeup desk. She considered her image in the small round mirror. Even though she had that clean, well scrubbed, satisfied look about her, she confessed she hadn't been able to rid herself of Jared Jacobs as easily as she had other aspects of her trip.

She tugged a thick robe around her body, basking in its warmth. She could track the man down, probably within hours, but should she? Kitty shook her head. She wasn't sure she should. And that indecisiveness bothered her more than anything. He was just a man, after all. One more cock hardly mattered.

She smiled at her frown in the mirror. It wasn't his cock she'd been imagining so recently, and so vividly. It was his mustache, his tongue, and his laughing eyes.

Didn't he take her seriously? If nothing else, she'd be taken seriously.

She reached for her makeup kit. She'd put off a decision about Jared Jacobs for another day or two. She'd learned early on not to be rash.

Brushing blush on her high cheekbones, she made one decision she'd been putting off for too long. She'd track down her business contacts who owned racehorses. She grinned at her reflection. Maybe that was the most important thing she'd brought back from Seattle—a commitment to her childhood dream of owning the next Seattle Slew.

CHAPTER TWO

The following morning, after meeting for two hours with her two staff assistants, Kitty stepped out into the main office area to find Maria Alvarez, her receptionist/secretary, grinning like the proverbial Cheshire cat.

"What is it?" she asked. "Did we get an unexpected offer on a property?"

Maria showed plenty of white teeth as she shook her head from side to side.

"A new client?"

Maria shrugged, her big brown eyes turning toward the empty desk between her and the entrance.

Kitty followed Maria's line of sight. She gasped when she saw the long stem yellow roses — then she brightened. "So you have an admirer?" She wasn't about to fall into the trap of saying Maria must have a new male admirer. She'd been down that embarrassing road once before. Maria welcomed lovers of both genders and didn't appreciate assumptions otherwise.

For her part, Kitty tried her best to accept everyone for who they were. But switch hitting had no appeal to her personally. Still, whoever had given Maria the bouquet had excellent taste — whether the giver was male or female.

"They're not for me," Maria chided. "They're for you."

"For me," Kitty squeaked. She stared hard at the flowers. They'd lost some of their luster. Who would be trying to butter her up with flowers? She wasn't easily overwhelmed by such sentimentality.

Cautiously, she approached the desk and reached for the tiny note card. Opening it, she frowned. The words had no meaning. She gulped. Yes, they did. It read:

> To the vision in yellow. Perhaps we should start over.
> JJ

Damn it. He'd gotten to her before she could make up her mind about him. At least he wasn't assuming anything. The roses, the card were a peace offering, of sorts. She nodded. He must be smiling over what she might do with the flowers. Did he expect her to toss them out, or accept them without comment?

She brought a yellow rosebud to her nose. She loved the fresh scent. Had he known she was a softie for flowers? Usually she had to buy her own.

"I can put them in water, if you like," Maria said.

Kitty glanced back at the fifty-two year old bursting with curiosity. "Please. It's nothing to get

20

too excited about."

Maria rose to her feet and beamed a warm smile. "I was giving it fifty-fifty that you'd toss the flowers in the waste basket. So I'll be a little excited for you."

Kitty walked back to her office and closed the door behind her. She sat at her desk and stared at the phone. What should she do? She'd dug up his work phone number as soon as she'd gotten to her office. Jared obviously had hers, too, since he had her work address.

Obtaining his home phone would take a little more doing. Hers wasn't going to be easy to get either, if he wanted it.

She shook her head at the phone. She'd promised herself a couple days to decide about the man from sunny California. Had he really seen her as a vision in yellow? She wet her lips. She had to admit she liked that—a lot.

- o -

Trimming his moustache after shaving, Jared wondered if his vision in yellow had received her flowers yet. He wasn't sure, but there was a two hour time difference.

He shrugged, trying to convince himself he was as nonchalant as he appeared in the mirror. What had he expected? A phone call dripping with thanks? That didn't seem like Kitty Paige's style.

Would she hang up on him if he called her?

Probably. It was too risky to try that. He had to soften her up more before taking that step. Though he'd sure love to hear her throaty voice again.

Before the day was over he'd have her home address and private phone number. He nodded at his own reflection. He'd already asked Sorenson to do the necessary digging. He knew he could trust the scrawny snoop. He'd used him on several cases. There had been times the man had ferreted out potential legal landmines resting beneath a company's surface before Jared had taken the fatal step of plunking down good money for it.

Jared glanced at his reflection and gave himself a satisfied smile. He'd be one step closer to claiming the vision in yellow before the day was done. He set the clippers down on the sink. "Patience," he muttered. He peeked down at the stiff erection tenting his pajama bottoms.

He shook his head. He didn't entirely like how much time the woman was taking. He was a busy man; he couldn't stand around all day thinking with his dick.

She'd better be worth the effort. He flashed on the image of her grinding away on his cock in the corner of the darkened ballroom and smiled — she'd be worth it.

He'd no doubt get over her in a flash, but she'd definitely be worth the effort.

Whistling to himself, Jared walked into his bedroom where he'd already laid out the day's clothes. It was time to select the next salvo for softening up Kitty Paige.

Was she fantasizing about him at all? He sure hoped so. He didn't like the thought of doing all the fantasizing.

What next? He didn't want to appear overly eager. He'd wait a week, but it wasn't too soon to consider his next step. He thought of Kitty's below-the-shoulder length blond hair. She'd worn it pouffed up for the wedding, with half of it falling over one shoulder and the rest down her back. It wasn't difficult at all to imagine drawing the blond tresses over a breast, using them to play hide and seek with a nipple.

Would her nipples harden quickly or would they rise slowly?

Jared tugged his trousers up over his arousal and tucked his shirt in. Carefully, he buckled the belt.

Did she ever wear her hair up? She'd look stunning with it up. Not that she didn't with it down.

He chuckled, toying with that image. A scarf. A yellow scarf. A yellow Thai silk scarf, like he'd seen in Bangkok. A long one, with long fringes. She could wear it around her forehead and let the tails fall down her back. Or she might lie naked on a bed and let the tails fall forward. Would they reach to her pussy, prompting another game of hide and seek?

His decision made, he reached for the bedside

phone to make the arrangements. He wished he could see her face when she'd seen the roses and the card. Damn, he wished he could see her when she ran the yellow silk scarf through her fingers. Would she appreciate its beauty? Would she run the pads of her fingers over it wishing she was running them over his flesh? Would her wrists tingle, aware the scarf would be perfect for binding them?

Jared jerked himself alert at the demanding voice on the phone. "Yes," he said at last, "I'm here. I'd like to place an order—a rush order."

- o -

The next morning Kitty immediately walked over to the yellow roses sitting on an end table next to the couch in her office. She sniffed and inhaled deeply. A smile crossed her lips. It was hard to forget Mr. Sunshine with these flowers greeting her. She imagined that was their purpose.

Sitting down at her desk, Kitty checked her calendar. Her morning was free. She was meeting for lunch with a couple who were interested in looking at houses in the million to million and half range—she grinned: her kind of client. There was a closing to attend in the late afternoon on a five acre parcel zoned commercial she'd brokered with a national retail chain.

She tapped her fingers on the desk. She really liked looking at her own investments grow, but she'd already decided her next investment was going to be a fun one. If it made money for her, fine, if not—so be it. Her commission from the retail chain would go a long way toward the purchase of a race horse.

The following afternoon Kitty stood in the alley of Barn B staring at the huge animal that was eyeing her carefully. She didn't know a lot about horses, but she had the same feeling she had when she stepped into majestic mansion with oak trim, French doors, and plenty of soft light. She recognized class and majesty even when it stood on four legs. Even when it snorted at her.

"As you can tell, he's a good looking animal. He'd be a good way for you to get started in horseracing. I'll make you a fair deal on a fifty-percent share."

Kitty nodded at her old friend and real estate magnate, Lawrence Madison. His white hair turned whiter each year. She'd been his broker almost from the time she'd broken into the business. Five years ago the man had been devastated by the death of his wife. Kitty had waited for more than a year before inviting him to her bed and showing him he still had much to offer a woman in her boudoir. They'd remained an item for over six months—a near record for Kitty. She'd done much to lift his spirits and reintroduce him to the world of the living. He'd taught her to appreciate older men. His staying power was phenomenal, particularly if she did most of the physical activity. They'd parted amiably after she introduced him to banker friend close to retirement. The two of them had been married nearly two years.

Lawrence thought he owed her. She smiled to herself. He didn't owe her a thing, but she knew she could trust him. And he'd been racing horses for over thirty years, making him the kind of partner she needed for her latest venture. She wanted to learn the business and she was a quick learner, but her old friend could coach her and guide her through the inevitable pitfalls of any business.

"I know you'll be fair, Lawrence." She didn't take her gaze off the horse. "So this fellow is four years old." She grinned at him. "Guess he's too old for the Derby."

The white-haired man chuckled and shook his head. "You'll probably get to the top of any business you decide you want to conquer, but we don't start there. If you want a derby possibility, we can visit one of the yearling sales later on and see what we can afford. For now, I'd advise tiptoeing into horseracing. This guy's no slouch. He's stakes quality. He has one win and two seconds in the five stakes he's entered. He'll be a contender." Lawrence gave her a sardonic grin. "That's about the best one can hope for—a contender."

She nodded. Her lips curved slightly. What

would her California man think of the horse? She pursed her lips. So was he a contender?

"He's still intact."

"What?" she looked sharply at Lawrence.

His face crinkled. "He's still got his essentials. He could become a stud—perhaps even a promising stud."

"Oh." Kitty wet her lips. "A promising stud. That would be nice."

"You've got that faraway look in your eyes, Kitty. Are we still talking about the horse?"

Kitty laughed easily and leaned over to peck his cheek. "You know me too well. Have the papers drawn up, Lawrence. How is Rebecca doing these days? I haven't seen her for weeks."

"She's doing fine. She told me to tell you she's excited about owning a horse with you. She wants us all to get together the next time he runs."

"When do you expect that to happen?"

"He bounced back from his last race nicely. We're shooting for a medium level stakes race here at Arlington in three weeks."

"Good. As soon as you know, let me know." She accepted his extended hand and shook it. "Thanks to both of you for your willingness to help me get started in this business. It's been a childhood dream I nearly forgot."

His fingers tightened around hers. "*We* thank *you*. For everything. And we'll help you learn the ropes. Like in any business, there are a lot of unsavory types who'd love to take advantage of newcomers—particularly a beautiful, wealthy woman. Do be careful."

She laughed. "I'll try."

"But not too careful." He winked. "Remember what I've always told you. You need to take more time for play. Maybe this four legged fellow can help with that."

Carefully, Kitty picked her way back down the alley. Her high heels clicking against the concrete echoed like gunfire. The next time she visited shed row she'd make a point of dressing more appropriately.

Warily, Kitty approached the small oblong box sitting on the spare office desk. A week had passed since the yellow roses had arrived, with no additional word from Jacobs. She'd almost given up on him, thinking the flowers might have only been a gesture of apology.

Maria had again called her to the outer office and without uttering a word pointed at the empty desk. This time Kitty knew better than to ask whether the package was a gift for her secretary.

She swallowed. Should she open it in front of Maria, or take it back to her office? Her breathing shortened. She didn't like Maria to make more out of these gifts than she should, but she didn't have a clue what Jared might send her next. And she knew it was from him. To be safe, she'd better retreat with it to her office.

Kitty ignored Maria's groan of protest as she

carried the box back into her office and closed the door.

She set the nicely wrapped box down on her coffee table and sat down on the couch. She eyed it carefully. "This is stupid," she muttered. The damn thing wasn't a bomb.

Quickly she tore the wrapping paper from the box and lifted the lid. She frowned and lifted out the yellow silk fabric. Her mouth fell open as she unfolded it to its full length. She stood and flung it around her neck. It was beautiful. It accentuated her hair coloring very nicely.

She reached for the card.

> *To my vision in yellow. In my mind's eye it is easy to see you dressed in this Thai silk scarf. I find it difficult not to wonder if you are as silky to the touch. May you think of me when you wear it.*
>   *JJ*

"Jesus," Kitty murmured, running her fingers over the silk. "This guy is good with words."

This at least answered one question. He was thinking about her. She smiled. He apparently had a rich imagination. Maybe he visualized her wearing nothing more than the yellow scarf. And he thought he might find her silky. Her loins warmed. Yes, that might be the case.

She twirled around lightly, sending the fringed tails of the scarf flying wildly. She laughed softly.

The scarf did have lots of possibilities. Had he considered tying her wrists with it and ravishing her? She smiled. That would be fine, as long as she could tie him up, too. She was typically such a control freak, but she did enjoy occasionally being out of control with a man who could satisfy her.

Kitty shook her head and inhaled sharply. She had work to do. Should she call him? She'd gotten his home phone. Maybe tonight. Her throat tightened. No. Not yet, anyway. She didn't have a name for the game they were playing, but they did seem to be playing one. Some men had tried to bribe her with gifts. This didn't feel like the same thing. Instead, he seemed to be enjoying playing a fantasy with her — or was it only with his vision in yellow? She could see his dark eyes laughing as he dangled possibilities before her.

When would he make his case for giving her the gift dangling between his legs? She moved toward her desk on shaky limbs. At the moment, he wouldn't have to argue that case very long at all. So how long would he shower gifts on his vision in yellow before one of them blinked?

She laughed aloud as an idea popped into her mind. She could play this game, too. Why should she wait around wondering what he might send her next?

- o -

Two days later, Jared strolled into the office

complex he'd built between his ranch house and the stables to find a small box resting on his office desk. Frowning, he hefted it. It hardly weighed anything at all.

He opened it gingerly and lifted the material between thumb and forefinger. He smiled broadly and then laughed hard. So his Kitty was into playing fantasy games, too.

He set the yellow thong aside and sifted through the paper until he found the note card.

> *To sunshine man with the thin mustache. Hope you don't mind that this is used. If you have a good nose, you'll likely discover my scent.*
> *K.P.*

Jared didn't hesitate. He drew the fabric to his nostrils. Yes, he could detect the unmistakable scent of a woman. So she had worn it. He peered at the yellow fabric closely. He'd never been so envious of an inanimate object. The large v-shaped panel had nestled against her pussy. The single corded strand of fabric had ridden in the crease of her ass. *Son of a bitch.*

Short of having her, it was the perfect gift.

Should he send her a third gift, or should he wait? Now that he knew she was playing the same game, he fully expected a second gift to arrive in the next day or two.

"Jared?"

He glanced quickly toward the doorway to see his buxom administrative assistant arching an eyebrow at the slightly used gift still sitting on his desk.

Serena Sampson's face broke into a wide grin. "I didn't know you were into collecting women's underwear. You haven't asked *me* for a contribution."

Jared hated to think he might be blushing in front of the redhead. She and her husband, who managed his ranch, had worked for him more than six years. He'd been fucking her since before she'd met Seth. He'd concurred with her choice for a husband, and Serena was right, he never had asked her for an undergarment. But then he hadn't asked Kitty, either.

"Hadn't occurred to me to start a collection," he drawled, regaining his composure, "until maybe now. So did you come in to tell me something, or to admire another woman's panties?"

Serena didn't even blush. "Your ten o'clock appointment has arrived." She tilted her head and peered down her nose over the top of her glasses. "I'll give you a few minutes to collect yourself. Do you need any help?"

"I'll be okay. And I'll come out and get Maxwell when I'm ready."

She nodded and retreated to the outer office, closing the door behind her.

Jared brought Kitty's thong to his nose and took one last sniff before putting it away. His vision in yellow had a flair for fun and games. He liked that—a lot. What would she come up with next?

Three days passed with Jared trying not to appear too eager for the mail to arrive. He knew Serena was more than a little curious why he was hanging around the office so much. On the third day he entered the office after returning from a town lunch and his smile broadened as he approached his desk. There sat a mysterious cigar shaped package.

He couldn't believe the slight tremble in his fingers and the catch in his throat as he tried to rip its wrapping off.

He lifted the box lid and howled at the simple yellow vibrator. He pulled it out and turned on its switch. It hummed. She'd even put batteries in it. Hopefully, she didn't think this would suffice as a substitute.

He saw a note card under the paper wrapping.

> To the sunshine man with the thin mustache. I have been told I'm quite silky. This, too, is slightly used. Feel free to use it however you see fit.
> KP

"Son of a bitch!" He dragged the vibrator under his nose before dropping it back in its box. They couldn't keep on like this. He'd have a heart attack if he had to open many more boxes from his vision in yellow.

He got up from the desk and looked out across the nearby paddock at several young colts and fillies at play. It didn't take long to reach a decision. He didn't care if it might look like he was caving in. What matter did that make? Besides, he'd been the one to start the game.

His trainer had shipped two horses to Arlington Park earlier in the week just in case some sort of excuse was needed. He picked up the yellow vibrator. Probably no excuses were needed or would be believed, but the horses might provide a cover for a little while.

He stepped out of his office and ignored Serena's questioning stare. "Serena, get me a ticket to Chicago. First flight you can get me on tomorrow."

"That'll cost a bundle."

"Doesn't matter. I have to get to Chicago."

"This Kitty woman has her hooks in you, doesn't she?" Serena didn't look troubled, just curious. "She must be something. I can't remember you ever getting this excited about a woman."

He tilted his head to the side and waited for her to correct her own observation.

"Well, with the exception of me, of course."

"Good girl," he said, leaning down to kiss her briefly. "Glad to see you're not losing your memory entirely. Wish me luck," he added, heading to the door. He needed to fill his lungs with the heavy stable air.

"Oh, I do," Serena quipped. "You know both Seth and I do. When do you want to return?"

He stopped and stared at the package he still clutched in his hand. "I hadn't thought about that. Leave the return open for now."

"Okay, boss. I'll get right on it." Serena blew him a kiss. "Have fun."

- o -

Frowning at the unfamiliar number on her caller I.D., Kitty nodded at the contractor she'd hired to do the rehab on a nineteen-twenties four-square she planned on reselling within the next six months. She'd been making the rounds of the four construction projects she had underway. It was her experience that if she didn't keep routine tabs on them, the projects slowed. Contractors often responded to the squeaky wheel.

She smiled as she carefully made her way across the sub-flooring, making sure her high heels resonated through the empty house. She knew that sound translated into power with most construction workers. As usual, she'd chosen her wardrobe with her day in mind. This was not a day for refined, potentially high-paying buyers. This was a day for making sure the men she hired didn't forget they were working for her. In addition to her blue high heels, she'd chosen a beaded pair of blue denim hip huggers and a simple canary yellow cardigan that failed to reach her jeans.

She avoided eye contact with the workers as she made her way to her car. She saw no need to embarrass them as they fantasized about her ass. One of her goals was to be the squeakiest wheel contractors ever heard. So far, she seemed to be meeting her goal.

She chuckled, leaned up against the car and glanced back toward the four-square. Men working on its siding quickly found something to do. Damn, she loved being a woman.

She punched a button on her cell, retrieving and returning the most recent call. Brushing her hair aside, Kitty brought the phone to her ear.

She startled when she heard the deep drawl.

"Wondered when you'd get back to me."

She stood taller and cleared her throat. She'd recognize his voice anywhere. She'd been thinking about it far too often. And now he'd called. What did he want? As if she didn't know.

"Hello," she said softly. "Fancy hearing from you."

"Thought maybe I should let you know I don't mind getting slightly used gifts."

She smiled broadly and idly watched a man climb a ladder and then move onto the roof of the four-square. "I'm glad. I doubt I have anything to offer that hasn't been used."

His sexy chuckle immediately pebbled her nipples. "That is appealing. I'm a man who prefers experience to naiveté."

Kitty began to pace, imagining Jared smoothing out his thin mustache. How long should she play with him? Should she invite him to Chicago? Maybe she ought to fly to San Diego. It did seem like they'd done enough dancing. She was ready to satisfy her curiosity about his mustache. Certainly he wouldn't have qualms about getting his precious mustache wet with a woman's juices?

"You busy this afternoon?"

The question and the soft chuckle jarred her to a standstill. "What?"

"You heard me. I've got a horse running in the seventh race. Should go off around four-twenty. If you could get here by then, you might bring me some good luck."

"Good luck?" She scowled. "Where the hell are you?"

"Oh, did I forget to tell you?" His voice crackled with mirth. "I'm sitting here at Arlington Park. So can you come out here for me?"

"Jesus," Kitty mumbled under her breath. "You expect me to drop everything and hustle out to Arlington?" She glanced at her watch. "There wouldn't even be time to go home and change."

"I wasn't expecting anything." He paused. "I was hoping. You can't be overdressed or underdressed at a track. Anything goes here. Are you wearing yellow?"

She smiled. "Matter of fact, I am. I'm wearing a yellow top."

"That's good enough for me. So are you going to come?"

She smacked her lips. She sure as hell wanted to. "If I leave the construction site now, and depending on traffic, I should make it by three. Will that be soon enough?"

"That'll be great. We'll grab a bite to eat after the races. I'll wait for you at the main entrance around three. Bye."

"I'll be there." She clicked her phone shut and puffed her cheeks up, then slowly released the air.

This was it. Damn, she loved the chase. She slid in behind the steering wheel. And she loved those initial bouts of lovemaking—getting to know a man's body and teaching a man what she liked.

She drove down the street a short distance and parked. She reached for her bag, pulled out a brush and ran it through her hair, then freshened her lipstick. She smiled at her reflection in the hand mirror. It would have to do. Hopefully he wasn't an old fashioned man turned off by hip huggers. Kitty smoothed out her top.

She tilted her head at her reflection and flashed an eyebrow. *What the hell.* She glanced around, discreetly slid her hands up under her cardigan, and unsnapped her bra. Laughing hard, she stuffed it in the glove compartment.

Kitty settled back behind the wheel and drove off. She was ready for the races. She was surprised he'd come to Chicago for her. The racehorses were an obvious ruse.

Now that he was here, she saw no point in sending him home without getting a little of what he hoped for. She checked her speedometer and slowed. It was difficult not to get excited about their next gift exchange.

CHAPTER THREE

"Hot damn," Jared mumbled as he recognized the tall blonde in hip huggers and a yellow top picking her way through other spectators towards where he stood.

He swallowed hard, his penis immediately springing to life. *Cripes.* He'd remembered her as a vision in yellow, but with sunshine bouncing off her pale hair and yellow top he was sure his eyes were playing tricks on him. Vision or real, he inhaled and rubbed his hands together. This woman was definitely worth the trip.

Her gaze never swayed from the doorway as she neared. She looked like a determined woman on a mission. He coughed slightly — he liked the idea that *he* was her mission. The only thing that bothered him was knowing she hadn't dressed that sexy specifically for him. So who the hell else was she trying to impress with her curves? Sorenson hadn't been able to identify a regular lover.

Whoever it was had better step aside while he was in town. He might tire of his women quickly, but he wasn't ready to share her. She'd be free to roam soon enough. He waved a beckoning hand at her. Smiling broadly, she waved back when she spied him. His heart skipped a beat. The damn woman made him feel half his age.

"Hi," she breathed, kissing him on the cheek. "I hope I'm not too underdressed for you."

He groaned and hugged her close, relishing the feel of her braless breasts crushing against his chest. He slid his hands down her spine until his fingers rested on her bare skin above her jeans. Even her skin felt warm like sunshine.

He blinked and broke away, taking her by hand. "Lady, I can't imagine you ever being too undressed for my tastes."

She squeezed his fingers without a hint of a blush. "We may have to see about that. So where is this horse I'm supposed to be a good luck charm for?"

He laughed easily. "Damn, it's good to see you. I've got a box reserved. My trainer doesn't like me to drop by before the race. He's sort of superstitious about that. He figures owners make the filly nervous."

"It's difficult to imagine you making a filly nervous." She smiled evenly and checked her watch. "So do you have a favorite in the next race?"

She made no effort to retrieve her hand from his as he guided her up a ramp to their box.

- o -

Kitty peeked at the man sitting next to her studying the *Daily Racing Form*. While she'd frequented the track often enough to know the *Form* was considered the biblical source for all things important about the horses on the day's racing card, she'd never bothered to learn how to read the coded numbers charting a horse's past performances. Given her recent purchase, she might need to master that arcane art.

Jared Jacobs wasn't fooling her by his apparent nonchalant attitude as he seemingly paid more attention to the *Form* than to her. His knee casually rested against her thigh. Was that his heartbeat or hers she could feel pounding where they touched?

His eyes had rounded when she'd drawn close enough for him to see her taut nipples pushing against the fabric holding them in. His fingers tracing the line of her jeans across the small of her exposed back had sent chills everywhere.

He liked her in yellow. Wasn't he lucky she'd chosen that particular top for the day? She hid her grin under her program. Maybe *she* was the lucky one.

He'd surprised her, too. The last time she'd seen him, he'd filled out a tux as well as any man she'd seen. He'd appeared suave, sophisticated, the master of his own destiny. This Jared was quite the contrast. From his western boots, to his form-fitting jeans, to his white shirt, to his corduroy sport coat, to his bolo tie, to his dark brown western hat, he exuded a breathtaking masculinity. She'd creamed almost as soon as she'd recognized him waving at her.

She inhaled deeply, catching a whiff of his cologne. *That* was the same, and so was his mustache. Again, she couldn't help but wonder if he took as much care with his women as he did with that mustache.

She was determined to find out. Soon. She glanced down the track to see the first horse entered in race seven make its way onto the track for the post parade. At least she'd made it in time for the big race. He hadn't complained about having to wait for her. She'd tried to get there as quickly as she could, but the traffic was atrocious.

"Is it number three I'm supposed to bring luck to?" She placed a hand on the inside of Jared's thigh half way between his knee and his crotch. She knew it was—Jared's name appeared in the program as owner of the number three horse.

He turned his head and gave her a devilish smile. "That, and number one," he said, reaching under his newspaper to slide her hand up to rest against his crotch.

Kitty wet her lips and held his gaze. He was definitely a right cock man. His rapidly growing bulge lay against her fingers. She wasn't about to back down from his daring. No one sat near their box—crowds were seldom huge on weekdays— and his paper screened his crotch from any prying eyes. She poked the tip of her tongue between her lips and curled her fingers around his now very alert penis. Her eyes must've given away her surprise at his size because Jared chuckled.

"You two weren't properly introduced the last time." He covered her hand, pinning it to his cock. "I hope you stick around for introductions this time."

Kitty didn't hesitate. She leaned over, brought her lips to his ear, and whispered, "I thought you only wanted me to come out here to bring your horse some luck." She dipped her tongue in his ear before settling back in her seat. Neither one of them did a thing to move her hand.

He raked his gaze slowly over her body, inhaled and shook his head. "Better keep your tongue to yourself, woman, or I'll drag you down to shedrow, find an empty horse stall and fuck you senseless."

Trying to ignore the burning sensations in her own body, Kitty smirked. "That's not exactly the ambiance I had in mind for our first time."

He opened his mouth as if to speak. They were both startled by the ringing of the starting gate and the call of the track announcer, "They're off."

Kitty jumped to her feet to stand alongside Jared. He wrapped an arm around her and held her tight. Was he afraid she was going to escape during the race? Not likely.

She laughed as Jared's horse moved to the front. She crossed her fingers, willing it not to look back. To her surprise, number three continued increasing her lead over the pack. By the time they reached the eight-pole, there was no doubt about the outcome. Number three won by seven lengths.

"Hot damn," Jared said, smiling broadly and taking her in his arms. "You *are* a lucky charm. She's good, but I've never seen her that good."

Kitty kept her eyes open as his mouth settled over hers. His were watching her with renewed intensity. She parted her lips and drew his tongue into her mouth. His hands cupped her jean-clad butt. This was intoxicating. She broke away, noting his surprise as well as her own. Their first kiss — what had she expected, something dull? The earth might not have been thrown off its axis, but to look at Jared, *he* might've been, and she wasn't at all certain about herself. She almost suggested they go find that horse stall.

"Do you want to see any more races?" she asked, squeezing his fingers.

He shook his head. His eyes twinkled. "What did you have in mind?"

"Do you have a car?"

"No, I came by limo."

"I'll drive."

"I'm staying at the Drake."

"We're not going there." She rose on her toes and kissed his chin. "It's time for me to collect my reward."

"Reward?"

"You didn't think good luck charms came without a price?"

He tipped back his head and chortled. "And you're going to exact payment, whether I'm willing or not."

She shook her head. "Oh," she said, looking as innocent as she could, "I do plan on being fair about this. I expect you won't be disappointed with your just desserts."

"Jesus," Jared growled, breaking their bantering spell. "Let's get the hell out of here. How long will it take to get to your place?"

"And I thought you were a patient man. My house is only about twenty minutes from here." She eyed his bulging jeans. "Thank goodness my car has bucket seats. Can't have you pawing me while I'm driving. Besides, you can keep your eyes peeled for cops."

"One eye," he corrected her. "The other is going to watch carefully to see if your nipples can grow any larger."

Fifteen minutes from the time they got into her Mercedes, they were clambering out of the car. Kitty fumbled with her keys but finally succeeded unlocking the front door. She led Jared into her grand entryway and closed the door on the outside world.

"Welcome to my house," she said, leaning against the door. She reached out and traced the length of his mustache. "Would you like a tour?"

He shook his head. His eyes darkened. "Not of the house. Later."

She undid the top button of his shirt. "Would you like a drink?"

Again he shook his head and kept his gaze on

her fingers as they moved to the next button. She watched him and undid one more button before lowering her head to nibble on his chest hairs.

"Damn," he muttered into her hair, "this is as good a spot as any."

She chuckled against his chest as he tried with little success to slip his fingers inside the back of her jeans. She reached between them to undo the snap. His hands immediately seized the advantage, sliding under her panties to cradle her rear. His fingers kneaded her butt cheeks and she purred against his pecs.

She used both hands to work on his buckle. This was proving to be a damn good spot. He might as well learn right away she didn't require lace and frills, not that she didn't enjoy them from time to time. She'd introduce him to her bedroom later. Right now there was a more important introduction she wanted to make.

With his buckle free, she fumbled with his zipper until she'd worked it down as far as it would go. She rested the top of her head against his chest and watched her hands slide out her reward. As expected, his cock was hard and thick. Her eyes rounded with pleasure when she unfurled its length. "Oh my," she moaned. "We are going to enjoy getting to know each other better."

She didn't bother with any more shirt buttons but slid his jeans down over his butt, giving herself an even better view. She encircled his cock with both hands and slid them slowly up its length, enjoying its feel and his gulping for air. Was a man ever more defenseless than when a woman had both hands around his cock?

She slid down his chest until she was eye level with his penis. His hands eased up her back, caressing her shoulders and neck. She rubbed a thumb over his cock's velvet head and smiled at the slight pressure Jared's fingers applied to her shoulders. He wasn't asking her for something she wasn't willing to give.

She flicked out her tongue, tapping the soft crown. Jared rose on his toes and settled back. She cradled his balls and ran her tongue the entire length of his shaft.

"Christ, woman!"

She giggled and drew the tip of his penis into her mouth. Jared's legs stiffened. She took more of him in and his fingers twined in her hair. She tried with little luck to relax her throat muscles. Another time, she'd see if she could take all of him. This time, she didn't think either of them wanted him to finish in her mouth. She moved up and down his shaft, wetting him thoroughly. She didn't have to worry about herself—she'd been creaming since they entered the house.

She quickened her pace until he grabbed her shoulders and hauled her up to face him. His cheeks had turned ruddy. Maybe he'd been closer than she'd thought. Or maybe he was simply running out of patience.

"Can you get rid of those jeans?" he asked gruffly. "I'll take care of my boots."

He never took his gaze off her as he stood on one leg to dispose of one boot and then the other.

She, in turn, waggled her butt and pushed the offending jeans down over her thighs and legs. She kicked the jeans aside and slipped her feet back in her high heels. She saw his eyes round. She expected the extra elevation might be helpful.

He kicked off his jeans and stood before her in all his glory. She reached out to steady his cock, but he shook his head. "What about those panties?"

"These little things?" she teased. She wiggled out of them, tossed them aside and stood in front of him, widening her stance to give him the best view possible. She watched him swallow hard.

"Jesus," he gasped. "Shaved bare."

"You must have twenty-twenty vision," she quipped. "She's ready and eager to meet you. She's been creaming much of the afternoon."

"Good," Jared said, dropping to he knees. "Let me introduce myself to the lady properly."

Kitty wasn't surprised when she felt his tongue gliding up and down the crease between her pussy lips. She groaned when the hand cupping her ass drew them tighter and his tongue explored the entry.

He hoisted her left leg over his shoulder and steadied her butt in his strong hands.

She sighed, pleased she'd put those shoes back

on. She cooed nonsense when he withdrew his tongue and rubbed his nose up and down her slit. His nose grazed her clit, threatening her sanity.

He chuckled.

Then she felt the hairs of his mustache skimming her clit. "Son of a bitch," she squealed, bearing down against his nose, his mustache, his chin — anything she could find.

His chuckles reached her ears before she felt his tongue probing her channel as deep as it could go. She flexed against it, and his fingers kneading her ass encouraged her. She humped his tongue madly, as if she'd never been tongue fucked before. He pawed her ass. A finger tapped on her anus and she flailed in his arms, losing track of everything but her shattering. She shuddered and gulped for air.

Jared slid off her pussy and brought her foot back to the floor. He stood and pressed his wet lips against her mouth.

Kitty tasted herself. Wrapping her arms around his neck, she broke away from the kiss and whispered, "That answers *that* question."

"What question is that?" he muttered against her cheek.

She curled her fingers around his erection and rubbed its head along the crease his tongue had so recently visited. "Uhm. I'd worried that a man who obviously spends so much time grooming his mustache might not want to get it wet with a woman's juices."

His laugh came immediately and deep. "I'm pleased we were able to dispel that worry." He lifted her chin. "But I'm afraid I'm completely out of patience. Kitty, I need to be in you." He reached in his pocket for a condom.

"I hoped that might be the case." She turned away from him to face the entryway door, leaned over, and braced her palms against the door. Looking over her shoulder and wiggling her butt, she asked, "See anything that might work for you?"

"Christ, you have a luscious ass," Jared said, coming up behind her.

She felt his cock tap against her butt. His hands parted her buttocks wide and his shaft slid down her crease. When it paused briefly near her anus, Jared leaned over and whispered, "Another time."

She tossed her head back. "I hope you're a man who keeps his promises."

"Oh, I do that," he murmured, parting her lips with one hand and guiding his cock head to her slit.

She gasped as it sought entry. He reached around to massage her labia, helping her widen to take him in. She struggled for enough air. She felt him sliding in, inching his way along her tight sleeve.

She chewed on her lower lip until at last his hips nestled against her ass. He was in. She had all of him.

"Damn, you are so hot and tight."

She propped herself up on one hand and reached underneath to cup his balls with the other. "I'll bet these guys are still holding onto my reward."

She quickly braced herself against the door with both hands. "What are you waiting for?"

"Not a damn thing," he growled, sliding his hands up under the yellow top she still wore until each hand cupped a breast.

She let out a small gasp. Like her, he still wore his shirt. She had started on it, but had never gotten it off him. There hadn't been time. He pulled almost all the way out of her. She gulped. There wasn't time for much at the moment but accepting his cock and what it had to offer.

He plunged back into her. Finesse, if it had ever crossed his mind or hers since they'd entered the house, was definitely gone. This was now a race to the finish.

Silently, he drove in and out of her. His tempo quickened.

Her thighs burned with anticipation. She felt him expand inside of her.

"Damn," he groaned.

"Go for it. Fill me."

He pinched her nipples. "Come with me," he demanded.

He might as well have had a direct track to her climax. She closed her eyes and opened them quickly. It was rising from her toes. She pounded the door with a fist when it reached the back of her knees. "Yes, yes, yes," she cried out, keeping time with his thrusts and her fist on the door.

She felt him jerking deep inside before he howled. He dropped his hands from her breasts and steadied himself on her hips but didn't stop pummeling her.

She never knew when he stopped. She'd lost track of him as her own internal explosion threatened to dismantle her cell by cell. She struggled for breath.

At some point Kitty became dimly aware Jared was no longer buried in her, but was gingerly helping her to the floor. For long moments they lay side by side on the carpeted entry way gasping for breath. Her eyes fluttered open and closed.

She smiled as he lightly kissed her eyelids. She caressed his mustache, still wet from her pleasure.

He nibbled on her ear. At last she opened her eyes. His look of satisfaction warmed her. "Welcome to my place," she whispered.

His smile was brilliant. "I should be ready for that house tour in about an hour or so."

She chuckled and cradled his head to her still-clad breasts.

"Next time, I'm going to want to see these. You have very responsive nipples."

"I'm sure they'll be happy to meet you up close and personal."

Two hours later, Jared watched Kitty bounce up and down on her bed, taking his cock deeper into her tight pussy with each thrust. He grabbed her nipples and pulled on them.

She ran her tongue across her upper lip. "You do seem to enjoy my tits," she said, smiling deliciously. She slowed her pace.

He leaned back to watch her breasts bounce up and down and from side to side. "They are as stunning as the rest of you."

"And you like my belly ring," she said, running a finger over the turquoise figure in her navel.

He nodded and tucked his hands behind his head. "I said I did." He grinned when she gave him a puzzled look. "He's all yours, lady. Do whatever you will with him. I'm sure you will anyway."

"Is that a complaint?" She came to a halt and squeezed her inner muscles around his shaft.

"Not hardly," he said, trying not to moan. He wanted her to know this was her show. They'd worked in concert in the entryway, then he'd been so bothered by her ass leading him up the sweeping stairway to the second floor he'd had to taste her again. If the stairs were uncomfortable for her, she hadn't complained. He'd slid up her body once he had his fill, and she'd licked her juices, still dribbling from his chin. And then she'd pushed him off her and continued conducting the house tour.

They hadn't gotten any farther than her bedroom, where she'd finished undressing him and he finally met her scrumptious breasts. So this was definitely her call.

"Am I wearing you out, old man?"

He gave her a crooked smile. "Doubt you could. Figured this was your turn. We might, though, kill each other off before either one of us cries uncle."

She beamed a broad smile at him. "You might be right about that."

He scowled when she rose above him and his cock fell from her warm sanctuary. "What the..."

She smirked but remained kneeling between his thighs. He watched her dip down to kiss the tip of his cock. He could handle that.

She straightened and sat back on her heels. She gave him a triumphant look. She had his full attention.

Then she encircled his cock with both hands and began to pump him slowly.

He swallowed. What the hell?

"I like to watch a guy spurt," she said by way of explanation. "With him watching. With him doing nothing but watching," she added, pushing an elbow against his thigh, which had begun to thrust with her.

"You love power, don't you," he grunted through clenched teeth as she continued slowly bringing him to the edge.

"Don't you?" She pouted. "Watching a man ejaculate is very powerful, I believe, for both partners. I won't get as much as you gave me downstairs — that would've been something to watch." She stuck her tongue out. "I really did enjoy that."

"Good," he gasped. "I'm sorry I won't have as much for you this time around."

"I know how to get the maximum amount out of a guy."

He watched her wet an index finger. He grinned when she squeezed his balls lightly and traced the ridge between his balls and his anus. He didn't try to keep his eyes from widening when she found his anus and entered.

She paused. "Do you like a woman's finger in your ass?"

"Yes."

"That's nice," she breathed, easing her finger farther as his outer ring opened under her insistence. "There's your prostate gland," she announced with pride, as if he might not have known where she was. "Hike your knees up a little."

He did, and she began fucking his ass, keeping time with her other hand on his cock. A groan escaped his lips. She stopped.

"Damn."

"Have you ever had a woman enjoy doing this for you as much as I am?"

He shook his head. There wasn't time to traipse

through his memory of all the women he'd known. Some had jerked him off, but he couldn't recall anyone, at least right away, who seemed to take such a perverse enjoyment in it.

Slowly she regained some pace. "Have you ever had a woman fuck you with her strap-on?"

He puffed air from his full cheeks and shook his head. Surely she didn't think they had time for another break. If she left him hanging, he'd have to finish himself off.

"Just asking," she said softly. "Hang around me long enough and I'll treat you."

Jared kept his fingers locked behind his head. He tried to think of anything but Kitty Paige wearing a strap-on.

She tilted forward, gripping his cock tighter. If anything, she managed to sink her finger deeper in his ass.

He swallowed hard as she became a blur. He was streaking toward a climax that might indeed rival the earlier one. He wasn't going to be responsible for his actions if she stopped again.

"He's coming," she squealed, "I can feel his surge building. There's the first drop." Her movements became smooth as she no doubt anticipated her reward.

"Come for me, baby," she cooed. Her finger rotated wildly in his butt. "Come for Kitty."

"You got him," Jared shouted, bucking against her movements. She made no effort to stop him this time.

"There he blows," she squealed.

He lost track of his initial spurts shooting high and then she leaned over, taking the rest of his come on her tits and belly. Her hands remained active until he shook his head. "There is no more," he growled. "Son of a bitch, you're some kind of a woman."

She chuckled before taking his slackening cock in her mouth to clean him. When she let him drop from her mouth and withdrew her finger from his butt, she rubbed his whiteness into her skin as if applying body lotion. "No one has ever accused me of being a man," she said playfully. She winked. "You surpassed my expectations. I didn't think you'd have that much left."

"You enjoy playing the bad girl, don't you?"

She stretched out across his chest and nipped at his chin. "How do you know I'm playing?"

"I don't, for sure. I'm guessing."

She propped herself up on an elbow and grinned. "And do you have a remedy for bad girls?" She waggled her butt suggestively.

He took the hint and swatted her bare butt with enough strength that she flinched. She leaped off him and off the bed. He frowned, certain he hadn't slapped her that hard.

"I'm going to take a shower and clean up." She held up her palm as he tried to stir. "Alone." She lifted the hand he'd used to spank her bottom to her lips and kissed its palm. "I do believe I'm going to enjoy playing bad girl with you again."

Jared watched the blonde disappear into the bathroom and close the door behind her. He threw his arm over his eyes and groaned softly. She was going to be a handful.

He'd expected her to push him some, but she was going beyond his expectations. If she wanted to play with him, he didn't mind the idea of playing with her.

Why was she so intent on shocking him? At least he thought that was what she was trying to do. Was she telling him he could have her body any way and every way, but that was it? Was she trying to make him think she was simply a woman who only thrived on the edge? He knew she was capable of much more—not that it really mattered to him. Still, he knew she was a woman of considerable depth beyond sexual prowess. She was an incredibly successful businessman. He knew her daughter, so he knew Kitty was a fine mother. He sighed. And she was damn inventive in bed.

He didn't mind being the current beneficiary of her talents, but it niggled at him that she seemed so protective of the rest of herself.

Kitty Paige was turning into a challenge in unanticipated ways. Jared studied the ceiling. Maybe that was part of the definition of a challenging woman—she was often doing the unexpected.

CHAPTER FOUR

Mid-morning, Jared snapped his laptop shut. Commodities were skyrocketing around the world — particularly copper, gold, and platinum. He yawned, giving his suite a once over. He didn't expect corporate spies to emerge from the woodwork, but he'd learned the hard way about corporate espionage.

His computer was as secure as money could buy. No one could be trusted, including hotel housekeeping staff. He locked his computer in a special wall safe.

How about lovers? He grunted an epithet. He'd learned that lesson the hard way, too. Repeatedly. They couldn't be trusted. Period.

He picked up the morning newspaper and flipped through it. Concentrating on the words proved difficult — not that the news was so bad. He leaned back briefly, closed his eyes and flexed his fingers.

Was Kitty Paige purposely trying to get under his skin? Damn, she was a dynamo — in and out of bed. She went hot and cold like a poorly made heating blanket. She hadn't invited him to stay the night. He wasn't about to ask. He'd finally called a taxi.

Looking perhaps a little awkward, she'd

explained she had an early closing to attend this morning. Maybe she did.

She seemed so protective. Of what? He didn't think he'd ever been with a more sexually aggressive woman than Kitty. She seemed to delight in being at least one step ahead of him. Did she really think she could shock him? And why would she want to?

Jared smoothed out his mustache. He might yet come up with a thing or two to surprise her.

She hadn't even indicated any surprise that he'd flown to Chicago. She had to know the horses were only a smokescreen to get close to her.

Close. Jared set the paper aside. He'd never forget the vision of his woman in yellow propped against the entryway door wiggling her lovely ass at him. He'd purposely not removed her yellow top. He'd dreamed so much about her wearing yellow, it seemed perfect that their first mating would take place with her in yellow.

He wet his lips remembering how her anus had been nearly as open to him as her pussy. She'd made it clear on the phone she had nothing to offer him that hadn't been used. He sighed heavily. She hadn't failed to excite him with the two orifices they'd already tried out. He was sure the third would be no less intoxicating.

And damn, that was part of what bothered him. Kitty Paige was intoxicating. She was a walking aphrodisiac, and he wanted more. He needed more. Damn it, he'd demand more.

want."

"No!" She lowered her voice. "It's not you. And there's no one else—at the moment."

"Sort of caught you between lovers, I guess."

"Something like that." She tilted her head to the side. She had to be careful. She could blow whatever they might have cooking with the wrong word or even look.

Mercifully their sandwiches arrived, giving her a little more time to collect her bearings. She watched him take a bite of his ham and cheese and held back a groan, remembering the feel of that mouth tugging on her pussy. *Damn. Damn. Damn.* She wasn't ready for him to fly back to California if he wanted to stay.

"Fridays are one of the busiest days," she explained. "It's a big day for new listings. Most banks are closed on the week end."

"And…" His lips twitched.

Could he possibly know how much that damn little moustache tormented her? "I have an open house for a few hours Sunday afternoon— otherwise my weekend is fairly clear, if you'd like to spend more time together."

"That's something, I suppose. So am I to be your houseguest, or do I commute from the hotel?"

She looked quickly down at her plate. He was teasing her—she liked the freedom of having her own space. And it was nice to know she had her place if things didn't go well.

66

But he wanted more than her mouth, her asshole, and her pussy. He wanted a small window into who the hell the woman was. He wasn't looking for anything long term—good God—but he prided himself that with few exceptions, the women he'd loved knew they'd been loved, for a time. Raw sex—superb sex— without some emotional bond, however fragile and temporary, was not enough. At least not for him. How could it be enough for Kitty?

He checked his watch. She'd agreed to meet him for lunch. That might mean they'd actually have a chance to talk about something other than sex.

Jared rose from the chair and chuckled at the irony. It was usually *he* who was trying to smooth talk his way into a woman's panties.

- o -

Kitty adjusted the dark sunglasses as she got out of her car. She smoothed out her canary yellow mid-thigh skirt and straightened the collar on the pale blue blouse. She paused to undo one more button, smacked her lips and then set off for the restaurant to meet Jared for lunch. The clack of her yellow high heels announced her arrival and her breasts bobbed freely with each lengthening stride. She grinned as men and women stared at her.

What did they see? What were they thinking?

63

Did they see a successful business woman? Did they see wealth? Did they see class? Did they see a hot woman on the prowl?

They see a whore!

Somewhat shaken, Kitty avoided stumbling. She paused, heaved a sigh and looked quickly around. *Fuck you, Daddy.* She hadn't heard his voice for years. She certainly didn't have to start that up again. She'd paid thousands of dollars to shrinks to erase those tapes from her brain. Why now?

She ran her fingers through her curls one more time, squared her shoulders, and stepped through the restaurant foyer. She immediately spied Jared waving at her from a corner booth. He stood when she approached the table. She grazed his cheek with her lips and took a seat across from him. Unsure whether the shock of hearing from her father again still registered in her eyes, she left her sunglasses in place. If that bothered Jared, he didn't say anything. Ever the gentleman. That was beginning to irk her. Was he ever *not* a gentleman? Even when he slapped her bottom, he'd done that with finesse.

"Busy morning?" he asked politely.

She nodded. "Harried. Things seldom go as planned."

"Or as they appear," he chimed in.

Was he alluding to her? She was too rattled to play games. Maybe she should've cancelled lunch. She placed the sunglasses on top of her head to read the menu. Blinking at the blurring words she fought for control. She'd make this a qui lunch. She had to get away so she could thir Should she call her shrink?

She glanced up at Jared, who seemed inten studying her every move. That didn't matter, matter what she or he wanted, she couldn't away with him this afternoon. She had thin take care of. She swallowed. She'd pay him tonight — if she hadn't freaked out by then.

After they placed their orders, Kitty set make her plans clear. "So will you be going track this afternoon?"

"You trying to get rid of me?" Jare remained passive and he waited for a resp

"No. Of course not," she stammered. that I'm terribly busy today." She pout didn't warn me you were going to show doorstep."

"Like a stray dog," he quipped. understand you're busy. Believe me, I l busy is. And you're right, maybe I called before I flew out here. But surprising you seemed to have lots of r

She reached across the small squeezed his fingers. "And I was su wet her lips. "Pleasantly surprised. B

"But you're terribly busy."

She nodded.

"Am I cutting in on some territory? I can get out of here, if t

She peered back at Jared. He sat there poised and cocky. She knew he was toying with her. He was daring her. *Damn him.*

She nodded her chin slowly. "House guest," but she quickly added, "only if you agree that you'll leave as any gentleman would if I ask you to."

He nodded. "The lady strikes a bargain. So you believe I'm a gentleman."

"Aren't you?" She couldn't decipher the emotion flickering across his dark eyes.

"You'll have to be the judge of that. So I understand you're a preacher's kid."

Kitty gulped and searched her purse for her smart phone. "I forgot to enter an appointment," she said with a slight tremble. When she finished with the entry, she stowed the phone back in her purse and lowered her sunglasses.

When she glanced back at Jared, he had that damn amused look on his face. "Oh," she said, as if she'd forgotten his question. "Yes, my dad was a preacher."

"That must've been like growing up in a fish bowl."

She shrugged her shoulders and picked at her French fries. "You get used to it."

"Yeah, like you can get used to anything." He leaned back in the booth and appraised her. "You must've been a handful when you were a teenager."

A chuckle broke her lips. "Long before that."

She scowled. "So how do you know so much about me?"

"I know your daughter, remember?"

"Oh." Her stomach clenched and her lungs froze. What had his son said — probably most every man attending the wedding would've slept with Susan. Good God! She'd never seriously thought Jared might've been one of those men.

She shoved her shaking fingers under the table. "I'm sorry," she said as calmly as she could, "but I really have to go. I can't think straight at the moment. There's just too much I have to do this afternoon."

Jared stood as she slid out of the booth. "So am I still invited to come by tonight? We could do dinner."

"Of course," she mumbled, not wanting to look at him directly. "I'll be ready by seven."

She scurried away from him. Her high heels no longer echoed power, but rather, retreat. By the time she reached her car, retreat sounded like a great idea. Retreat from her work, retreat from her daddy, retreat from Jared. But she knew from experience she could never retreat from herself.

She'd made one decision on the way out of the restaurant. Before she gave herself to Jared again she'd know whether he'd fucked her daughter. If he had, she'd pay for the taxi that'd take him out of her life.

- o -

Back in the restaurant, Jared nibbled on a French fry, not at all certain he fully understood what had just transpired. Kitty had been strung like a taut banjo when she'd joined him. He did understand how days could get away from you.

He scowled at the door she'd just gone thorough. Not everyone trusted him. That was a fact of life. He'd earned distrust often enough, but what the hell had he done to Kitty Paige to earn hers? He'd romanced her from a distance and then had shown up—admittedly, unannounced. She'd certainly seemed eager to please him last evening.

Was she having morning-after thoughts? Wasn't it rather adolescent to try to hide behind shades? And why such a tortuous response to his simple question about growing up a preacher's kid? He'd had a buddy in high school who'd been a preacher's kid. Clearly he'd seen some pluses, but there were also the obvious minuses of church people expecting the kid to be a saint.

He smiled. Somehow he didn't think Kitty had ever been confused with a saint. He raked his fingers through his hair. Maybe his question hadn't been so simple. Her family probably hadn't been overly pleased with the daughter becoming an out-of-wedlock teenage mother. But they must've gotten their heads around that. Susan had turned out to be a delightful young woman. Surely, Kitty must have had lots of support raising the girl.

Jared smoothed out his mustache. He hadn't meant to pry. He'd thought they'd share some small talk. He'd ask her about her childhood days and she'd ask about his, and then they'd move on. Simple. Apparently, not.

He reached for the bill and glanced at his watch. He'd already missed the opening race, but he'd head out to Arlington anyway. That was closer to where he expected to spend the night.

He smiled. That was definitely one thing to look forward to. He hoped Kitty didn't wake up in a foul mood every morning.

Precisely at seven that evening, Jared rang her doorbell. He tried to hide his surprise when she opened the door. She stood in front of him with the most helpless, forlorn look. She was hardly dressed for going out to dinner, or for seduction. She wore yellow shorts and a paint splattered man's shirt.

Silently, she led him directly to the kitchen. It was only then that he noticed she was barefoot. No high heels. No nothing. She probably had no idea how sexy she looked in those tattered clothes with bare feet. He used extreme control not to lay her over the dining table. She didn't look like a woman with love on her mind.

She poured them each a cup of coffee. He figured he could use something stronger than that.

"Sit," she ordered. "We need to talk."

He sat. It was never wise to argue with a woman until he knew what the hell she was going to argue about.

Kitty remained standing. Her hands trembled slightly as they brought her coffee mug to her lips. She set the mug on the table and laced her fingers at her waist. "I don't know how else to ask. So I'll just ask you straight up. Have you fucked my daughter?"

"What?" Jared was on his feet before he could think.

Kitty took a step back and shot him a wary look.

"Jesus H. Christ, is that why you were so wired this noon? Why didn't you ask me last night?"

"I didn't fucking think about it last night!" She swallowed. "I'm asking now. Did you fuck Susan?"

He shook his head vigorously. "I don't have time for college girls. I like my women a little older," he paused, "and hopefully a little wiser. Why in hell would you ask such a question?"

"Your son," she stammered. "Jackson told me Susan had slept with most every man who would be attending the wedding."

He took a step forward. She didn't retreat this time. He reached out and cupped her chin. He ran his thumb across her lips. "Did you wonder about that when we danced at the reception?"

She glanced down at her toes. "The question crossed my mind."

"And you still led me on."

"Not on purpose. I knew I had the redeye to catch."

"Right. And then you conveniently forgot about your daughter until after you had a chance to sample what I was offering. Are you trying to get rid of me?"

"No. That's not it. I'd forgotten about Susan until this morning."

He placed his hands on her shoulders. She showed no sign of resistance. He crushed his mouth against hers and ground his body against hers until she began to respond in kind. He slid his lips off, cupped his hands over her curvy ass and ground her yellow-clad crotch against his erection. He nodded when she adjusted her fit until he was certain she had him where she wanted him. "And what were you planning on doing if I said I had fucked Susan?"

Her eyes glazed and she worked her lips with effort. "Sending you away."

"Really? You could've walked away from this?" He hoisted her legs until he held her butt in his hands and she locked her legs behind his back.

"Yes," she panted, gliding up and down his cock through the fabric. She bit his shoulder. "Oh, God. Why are you doing this to me? Oh God, I can't stop. I'm coming."

She clasped her arms around his neck and tightened the grip of her legs. He held her steady, letting her body quake against his. He held her until his arms screamed for help. At last, she tried to find the floor with her feet.

Kitty took a step back from him and wiped her mouth with the back of her hand. Her eyes still seemed out of focus. "Why?" she reiterated.

Jared filled his chest with air and steadied his own pulse. "I need you to know I'm a damn difficult man to get rid of until I'm ready to go."

"And you're not ready."

He shook his head and watched her lips curve up into a half-smile. "Sometimes you can be quite perceptive. You do believe me—about Susan?"

She nodded. "You wouldn't lie about that."

"That doesn't sound like a total vote of confidence."

She shrugged. "I don't know you that well."

He grimaced. "Maybe we should do something about that. Anyway, since we're talking about our children, let's get one more out of the way."

Kitty shrank from him. "Jackson."

"Jackson. So do I care that you fucked Jackson—apparently you would've cared some, at least, if I'd gotten it on with your daughter. The answer is hell, no. He's an adult. You were an adult. Just for the record, if I had hooked up with Susan, I would've hoped you could've remembered that. But," he held up his palm to prevent Kitty's interruption, "that didn't happen. I gather from what you said at the wedding reception, Jackson didn't exactly ring your chimes."

73

Kitty wet her lips and swallowed but didn't try to speak.

"I apologize for that," Jared continued. "He should know how to treat a woman by now. And don't trust everything the boy says. Jackson is noted for exaggeration. I don't doubt she's been with a number of guys, including my son, but I highly doubt I was the only man at the wedding who hadn't screwed her."

She continued to look at him wide-eyed and open mouthed.

He placed a finger under her chin and closed her mouth. "Do you suppose we have any more need to talk about our children's love lives?"

"Do you and your son often talk about your women?"

He smiled at the renewed fire in her eyes. His Kitty was coming back from wherever the hell she'd been most of the day. "I never talk with him about my women. Occasionally, when he gets sloshed enough, he volunteers stuff I don't particularly want to know."

"So would you have been attracted to me if he hadn't told you I was hot?"

"You've got to be kidding. I didn't need a twenty-two year old to tell me you were going to be hot, in bed or out. You exude heat, woman. Do you have any idea how hot you were walking your daughter down the aisle of that church?"

She shook her head.

"I felt sorry for Susan. Every one knew she was

taken. But you? Hell, even the preacher had to struggle to find his place in his script after he watched you come down that aisle."

She smirked. "I do recall a longer pause than I remembered during rehearsal." She rose on her toes and nibbled on his chin. "So who knew you could be good for a woman's ego?"

He pulled her body in tight to his and inhaled her scent. "I have my moments. Don't get too used to it."

"I won't," she murmured. She leaned back against his arms. "Now that we've cleared the air, I'm famished."

He gave her a crooked smile.

"Not that," she said quickly. "Maybe later. I have a favorite Italian restaurant not too far away. Will that work for you?"

"That works for me." His gaze traveled slowly down her body. "Are you going to put on shoes?"

She tapped his chest and winced. "I'm not going out looking like this. Give me a few minutes and I'll be ready." She waved over her shoulder. "I won't be long, really."

He nodded and then warmed up his coffee before sitting back down at the table. She didn't strike him as a woman who could ever dress in a hurry.

He leaned back and blew air through his compressed lips. That was close. At least he had some idea what moved her in addition to passionate sex. Her daughter.

Jared closed his eyes. He hadn't lied to her. He hadn't fucked her daughter. He did have a rule against younger women. That didn't mean Susan hadn't tried to hook up with him.

She'd been as bold as her mother. He'd been over at her husband-to-be's place for dinner and to tutor Brad in the use of a new software business program when Brad had dashed a term paper over to a professor's house. Brad's car had hardly left the driveway before Susan started making her moves.

He'd told her no. He'd told her about his rules against younger women. Put out and exasperated, she'd strutted to within three feet of him, calmly lifted her short skirt and proceeded to bring herself off. She'd been commando. When she came, she wiped her sticky fingers on his shirt saying he'd better remember her five or ten years later when she tracked him down.

Jared shook his head. Susan would be one pissed off woman if she knew he and her mother had hooked up.

- o -

Feeling much relieved, Kitty hummed while dressing for her evening with Jared. She might not have been coy about it, but at least her fundamental question got answered. Jared hadn't slept with her daughter.

She shivered, recalling the scene in the kitchen.

Oddly, they'd finished what they couldn't in the hotel lobby at the wedding reception. This time he'd purposely pushed her over the edge to prove a point. He'd had no intention of letting her down until she came. As he said, she wasn't going to get rid of him easily without his agreement.

She freshened her lipstick. Not that she had any plans on dispatching him anytime soon. Even her emergency phone consultation with her therapist had helped, though sometimes she thought her therapist might be more wacked out than she was. It was good to hear Sandra Aster's calming voice on the line. Sandra had reminded her of some of the devices she'd learned to avoid getting hooked by her father's voice. After all, the man had been dead for nearly a decade, but the tapes spinning her memory could be as powerful as ever.

She'd go back to using some of the self-talk messages she and Sandra had worked on over the years. She'd look at pictures of her father to remind herself that he was only flesh and blood and that he seldom looked happy, whether he'd been lecturing her, eating at a barbecue, or even preaching. Her father had been a deeply unhappy man. That was the case both before she was born and after. She'd really had little to do with his unhappiness. But she did have to be reminded of that fact from time to time.

But why now? Why would her father pop up after being absent from her thoughts for years?

Kitty chuckled, shrugged into a white men's

dress shirt and tied a knot under her breasts, leaving a clear view of her belly ring. What was the point of having one if you didn't show it off now and then?

She slipped into a string bikini bottom and reached for a yellow skirt. Maybe Jared was right. She did have a proclivity for wearing yellow.

But Sandra was way off base about Jared. Sandra's response to the sudden intrusion of her daddy's voice was to ask if there was a new man in her life. They'd gone over her teen years not long after she and Sandra began working on her crap. Her dad always got furiously jealous if she dated a guy more than twice. He thought they were getting serious.

And she had spent a lot of time fantasizing about each boy. Was this the one she'd live out her days with? Maybe she *had* been serious, in a young girl's fanciful way.

That was her daddy's problem—though he'd been quite adept at making his problem hers, including complaining to the boys' parents that he feared the devil might lead them astray. She smiled. By the time she and Todd got together later in high school, she no longer told her parents when she would be with a boy. Dates just happened. She'd made up for lost time learning about sex. And then she'd gotten pregnant. Maybe there *was* a devil.

According to her daddy, *she'd* been the devil. She preferred to think of the devil as having a cock.

She slipped her feet into her reliable yellow high heels. She grinned, imagining Jared with horns. Certainly the devil must have a thin mustache. Everyone knew that.

But Sandra was wrong about him. Her father didn't pop into her consciousness every time she took on a new lover. And she wasn't at all serious about Jared Jacobs, no matter what Sandra might hypothesize. She wasn't going to get serious about anyone, and certainly not about a man she hardly knew.

Satisfied with what she saw in the mirror, Kitty ran a brush through her hair and headed downstairs whistling softly. The image of Jared Jacobs as the devil incarnate did have more than a little appeal for her.

CHAPTER FIVE

"I love pizza," Jared said, grinning as Kitty tried to discreetly chew off the end of a gooey piece. It stuck to her chin. He peeled it off for her and she didn't hesitate to lick his finger clean. "Don't apologize for bringing me here. I'm sure their shrimp scampi is good, but isn't Chicago famous for its pizza? Besides, this is more fun. Your mood seems much lighter than it was at noon."

"It is," she admitted. "You had more than a little to do with that. She secured several small sausage slices to her pizza before lifting it toward her mouth. "So why the western hat? Does that simply signify you live west of the Mississippi?" Suddenly she gasped for air and waved frantically at her open mouth.

He laughed. "Some of those pieces are hotter than others. Actually, I've earned the hat."

Her brow furrowed. "How's that? I've heard of cowboys earning their spurs, but not hats."

He wondered how many cowboys she'd known. "I actually live on a working ranch."

"You do?" Her brow furrowed delightfully. "I thought you lived in San Diego, where the sun shines all the time."

"Not far from San Diego. Up in the foothills

east of the city. It's not a large ranch, by any means. Twelve hundred acres, give or take."

Her mouth gaped. "Give or take. Damn, that's a lot of land by Midwestern standards."

"Maybe Midwesterners ought to rethink their standards." He flashed an eyebrow and her cheeks turned a little rosy. Surprisingly, he liked having that effect on her. "I don't actually work the ranch myself. Like I said, I'm into commodities. I have a manager who operates the ranch for me. The race horses, of course, but we also run some beef cattle, and the obligatory small herd of cattle horses."

"A cowboy isn't a cowboy without his horse," Kitty teased. "I assume you ride."

"I'm told I'm a fairly good rider." He lifted a piece of pizza for her.

"I have no complaints," she said before letting him feed her.

"I hope you wouldn't. You're a superb rider, yourself." She arched her eyebrows and he smirked. "So do you ride horses?"

"Nope." She shook her head and mocked him. "Guess I'm into more specialized riding. Did I tell you I bought a horse?"

He did a double take. "No, you didn't mention it."

"Well, half a horse, really," she added. "Half of a race horse."

"A race horse. Well, I'll be damned. You are full of surprises. When did this happen?"

"Last week. I have an old friend who thinks he

owes me."

"I see—an old lover."

"Lawrence is happily married to a woman I set him up with. He's old enough to be my father."

"But still, a former lover."

"I'm not talking about old lovers, and I don't expect you to, either."

"Point taken. Okay, so this old infirmed codger wants to help a much younger woman find her way in the horseracing world."

She giggled.

He'd seldom heard her actually giggle.

"He's not that decrepit. And I own the horse with Lawrence and Rebecca. Rebecca is one of my few good friends."

"I see. All work and no play…"

"Something like that. So do you want to hear about this horse?"

"Tell me," he said, chuckling. "You're dying to."

"Well, I'm quite impressed. He's won at the stakes level."

"Really."

"Uh, huh. And I may not know much about riding horses, but I do know something about horseracing. I know stakes racing is where you're going to find your quality horses."

He nodded, giving her a half smile. "I'm not at all surprised you know quality when you see it."

She winced but otherwise ignored his comment. "He's handsome. Tall. Majestic. And has the darkest eyes."

"So does he have a mustache?"

"You," she snorted in a most unladylike way. "Not everything I say has to do with you." She paused. "Well, most everything."

"Maybe you can show me this new fellow of yours if we run out to the track tomorrow."

"That'd be great. Maybe Lawrence and Rebecca will be there. They often are, on the weekends."

"Looks like we've about polished off this pizza," Jared said, lifting his beer stein to his lips. "You have any more thoughts about the evening?"

She didn't miss a beat. "All of this talk about riding is making me want to get back in the saddle again. How about you?"

"Oh, I aim to please the lady. If we were at my ranch, I could put you astride a horse and teach you."

"But we're not at your ranch. We'll just have to make do with whatever substitute we can find." She ran a finger along the back of his hand. "So are you volunteering to be my horse *and* my cowboy?"

"Yes, ma'am, whatever you'd like me to be."

- o -

An hour later, Kitty threw one hand high above her head and laughed at their reflection in the wall mirror. "How am I doing?" They were on her bedroom carpet and she was indeed riding Jared as he knelt on all fours, carrying the bulk of her weight. His dark western hat was askew on the top of her head.

He beamed at her in the mirror. "Ride 'em, cowgirl!"

She bit down on her lower lip and dragged her wet pussy lips up and down the base of his spine, struggling for self-control. She narrowed her eyes at his reflection and tried to breathe.

He nodded. "Go for it, cowgirl. Dismount if you must. Rub your pussy all over my ass."

She stood and trailed her pussy across one butt cheek, then the other. His words triggered her.

"Go for it, girl. Claw your clit. Fuck my ass."

"Ah," she groaned, stroking her clit. She was so close, but she wanted to ride her cowboy. She curled both hands on his shoulder and stretched over his back, bringing her pussy to the top of his ass. She started slowly, but couldn't stay at that pace for long. She hurtled her loins against his ass. He grunted beneath her. The friction on her pussy became nearly unbearable—then she came. She came hard. "Jesus," she yelped, unable to stop.

"Keep coming," he urged. "I can feel your juices flowing down the crack of my ass."

"Cripes," she breathed at last. She kissed his head, his neck, his shoulders.

He laughed and lowered himself to the floor with her clinging to his back. "You ride real fine."

Smiling, she snuggled against his neck. She wasn't sure what she'd gotten herself into with

Jared, but she'd sure enjoy the ride while it lasted.

"He's a handsome specimen of the male animal," Rebecca Madison whispered in Kitty's ear.

Given that Rebecca seemed more interested in assessing Jared than the horse a groom was walking back and forth in front of the four of them, Kitty didn't have to guess about the object of the woman's praise. "He is that," she agreed in a low breath. "Well put together, and moves nicely."

"You've got a classy racehorse in that one, Kitty," Jared said, gesturing at the rear of the horse walking away from them. "Well conformed and moves fluidly." His gaze met hers and his eyes sparkled. "He'll bring you lots of pleasure if you stick with him. I expect you'll know what it feels like to be in the winner's circle."

"And there isn't much better than that," Lawrence chimed in. "What the hell are you laughing at?" he asked his wife, who had caught a case of the giggles. "You okay?"

"I'm doing fine, but I believe we've bragged up Rocketman enough. Jared was going to show us his filly, weren't you?"

"I've asked the groom to bring her out. She's in the next barn over."

Kitty watched Jared puff with pride as he looked toward the alley way. This man was into his horses. She followed his line of sight and saw the familiar groom leading a high stepping chestnut toward them. The haughty animal tossed her head from side to side, pranced and then settled, letting Jared run his hands up and down her legs. Kitty knew he was double checking for hot spots in her knees and tendons. The groom had likely done that first thing in the morning. The trainer would've followed suit, and now the owner. One could never be too cautious with a racehorse.

"Do you like her?" Jared asked, glancing up at Kitty while checking a front hoof.

"She's stunning—almost red in color, but she seems to have a mind of her own."

"That's the way I like my women," Jared quipped, standing to massage the filly's shoulders. "She'll run her heart out for me."

Kitty stepped back quickly when the filly bared her teeth.

"Don't mind her," Jared said. "She won't bite. She's a tease. What she's really looking for is attention and a treat." Jared reached into his jacket pocket. "Here, give her a couple of these and she'll be your friend forever."

Kitty took three small carrots from Jared's hand. She eyed the filly, whose attention was now focused on her. "You going to be a good girl?" She laid a carrot in the palm of her hand and let the filly scarf it up with her tongue. She'd already learned not to put her fingers in a horse's mouth—

they did have sharp teeth and strong jaws. Temporarily satisfied, the filly raised her head and nodded, looking for the other carrots.

"You're a smart one, aren't you?" Kitty offered her the second carrot and then the third. "I bet you turn all the guys' heads." The filly pranced from side to side.

"Careful," Jared cautioned. "She hasn't worked yet this morning. She's up on her toes. She really likes to race. She loves competition, but she'll have to wait couple more weeks for that. So when did you say your guy was running next?" he asked, looking at Lawrence.

"We have him nominated for a stakes coming up next weekend. If all goes well, he'll be in it."

Jared chuckled and nodded at the groom to take the filly back to her stall. "*If all goes well* is the mantra of horse folks." He frowned at his filly disappearing down the alley. "Keeping them healthy and willing isn't an easy task. I don't envy the trainer his job."

"Me either."

"So do you plan on using Rocketman at stud?"

Lawrence shrugged. "Hope to. He's competitive in grade two and three stakes. That's enough for some people. I'd like to see him at least place in a grade one before going too far with that dream."

"He's got an excellent pedigree," Jared offered. "You can't underestimate good breeding when making that choice. I know the track record is important, but I'll take a chance on generations of good breeding, even without the most stellar race record. It can be terribly disappointing and a huge drain of money to back a top race horse and then find he's a wimp in the breeding shed."

"Sounds like you might be interested in my stud," Kitty said, unable to contain her amusement, "for your filly. Wouldn't that be a hoot?"

"I don't see the humor," Jared said quickly. "They're a well matched pair on paper. His temperament is a little less fiery, a little less flighty. But they both have super conformation, good bone, and I expect they're both poetry in motion on the track."

Kitty flashed an eyebrow at Jared, who seemed to be thinking only about horses. He cast her a confused look, scowled, then blushed profusely.

Lawrence and Rebecca both laughed.

Jared huffed, apparently looking for some appropriate comeback.

"Come on," Kitty said, before he could dig himself a deeper hole. "Let's go see some races. Breeding prospects can be considered at a later time. I feel like a winner today, don't you?"

"Right," Jared drawled, letting her lead them back toward the stands.

Kitty didn't bother trying to explain the extra little bounce in her step. She enjoyed sharing Jared with her friends. They all seemed to hit it off quite nicely. Of course, they shared a common interest in horses.

She gave Jared a sidelong glance. His breathing had returned to normal. Did he wonder if his passion for horses had gotten him in trouble with her? Clearly, while some of the earlier discussion might've been tongue-in-cheek at times, his assessment of breeding prospects was purely horsey. He hadn't been playing to her. He'd been seriously weighing the merits of a particular match between her stud and his filly.

What had he thought when he realized his audience was traveling down two paths at the same time?

She hoped he appreciated being rescued from any more embarrassment. She wasn't looking for breeding prospects. She grinned. If she *was* looking for a stud, Jared Jacobs would fill the bill quite nicely.

She interlaced their fingers. His gripped hers strongly. She wondered if he was having similar thoughts. *Hers* were crystal clear and focused: how long would they have to remain at the track before she could take her stud back to bed and let him ravish her?

- o -

"That tickles," Kitty squealed, clearly not trying at all to hide her broad smile.

"I thought it might," Jared said, letting the fringe of the long yellow Thai silk scarf draped around her neck graze the taut nipple of one breast.

"Don't ignore the other one."

"I don't intend to." He let the scarf dip in her cleavage. He laughed when her eyes rounded, then he let the sash rest against the other breast before dragging it up and over the hard nipple.

"Torture," Kitty purred. "But sweet torture."

He nodded. Slowly, he dragged the end of the scarf down the centerline of her chest and belly, pausing to tease her belly button before proceeding lower. Kitty gulped for air as he brushed and re-brushed the sensitive line between her navel and the apex of her pubis. He smiled when he heard her soft moans and watched her labia swelling, expanding and opening just enough to provide him with a pinkish view.

She was primed, but not as primed as he wanted her.

Laughing as Kitty suggestively tilted her pelvis, he shook his head, avoided direct contact with her pussy and guided the silk down the length of one thigh and leg. She tensed and relaxed under his silky assault.

He held both ends of the silken sash in his hand, wrapped her foot, and massaged first one toe and then the next. Her squeals intensified. She stuck her tongue out. He moved to the second foot and gave it a silken massage also.

"Cripes, I'm exhausted, and you haven't even gotten there yet."

"Is the lady protesting?" Jared eased the scarf back up toward the long-intended target.

"Nooo. Not at all. You're wonderful, you know."

"A woman will say anything when she wants a man to please her." Her labia glistened by the time he let the silk fringes settle between her engorged lips.

"Oh, God. Have mercy."

"Not this time, babe." Jared easily lifted her butt and slid one end of the scarf under it. Quickly, he had her loins encased in silk and handed the ends of the scarf to her care. "I won't be needing these for awhile. You may find a use for them."

Her fingers curled around the scarf and he settled between her legs. He laved the silk around the edges of her pussy and then looked up with a grin. "Isn't it amazing how silk feels when it gets wet—your juices and my tongue."

She tugged on the silk scarf, increasing the pressure against her loins, and nodded jerkily. "Make me come, Jared."

"Like this?" He tongued the silk covering her pussy and pushed a little inside her folds.

"Oh, yeah. That'll do it. A little more."

He lifted his head and shook it when he saw her distressed glower. "Not yet," he whispered, retrieving the scarf. "Not nearly yet. You won't come until I'm ready for you to come."

He laughed as her gaze burned into him. He

grabbed her wrist and tied one end of the scarf loosely around it. Her eyes rounded with awareness. Her lower lip trembled slightly when he tied the overlap of the knot around a bedpost. She didn't move when he reached for her other wrist. "You know what I'm going to do?"

She nodded. "You're going to ravish me." She turned to watch him secure the second wrist.

He settled back to kneel between her legs and appreciate the view. "I knew you'd look gorgeous bound with that scarf."

"Is this why you bought it for me?" she asked, testing the knots by pulling a little.

He smiled and tugged on his mustache. "Oh, I figured it'd have lots of uses, but mainly it reminded me of you. I'll never forget this image of you splayed out waiting for me to make you come." He worked his hand slowly up and down the length of his cock. "Are you ready for this?"

"You know I am," she grunted. "Past ready."

"Am I going too slow for you? Too bad you can't hurry things along by strumming your clit." He grinned as her fingers curled and uncurled.

He slid his cock up and down her slick crevice. She rocked her pelvis, demanding more. He shook his head. "Don't try to tell me what to do. The more you try to help, the longer it'll take. Understand?"

She nodded.

He didn't know she could look so meek. "That's better. Be a good girl and I'll give you what you

want."

He pressed inward, sinking his cock into her vaginal heat. She gasped. He never paused until he was seated in her depths. She began to raise her legs and he shook his head *no*. "Do I have to tie your feet, too?"

"No," she whispered, stretching out prone beneath him.

"That's better. If I want you to join in, I'll let you know." He gave her a half smile. "You are loving this, aren't you?"

"Nearly as much as I'll love tying you up."

"Easy, woman, don't tempt fate while you're tied up. That's not a good strategy. Now where was I? Oh, yes," he said, leaning forward to hover above her with his weight on his extended palms and arms. He dipped his head to kiss one nipple and then the other. Kitty cooed with each touch and he was somewhat surprised she made no more effort to encourage his progress with her legs.

"Open your mouth," he demanded.

Wide-eyed, she complied. He teased the roof of her mouth with his tongue and rotated his cockhead from side to side just inside her vagina. He swallowed her gasp and then drove his tongue and cock deeper. He watched her eyes blink shut and open just as quickly as he drove in and out of her mouth and pussy.

Stopping abruptly, he lifted his head and winked. "That was close."

Her glower assured him he was right. "I could pull out of your pussy and finish in your mouth. Would you like me to fuck your mouth while your hands are tied?"

"Whatever you want."

He flexed in and out of her a few more times before stopping. "Or I could finish in your ass. You've been wanting me to do that, haven't you?"

"Yes."

"Or I could let you come right where I am." He settled back on his knees. He grazed a finger along the side of her exposed clit. "The French are fond of calling this a woman's petite erection." He stroked it between thumb and forefinger. "If I do this long enough, will you come for me?"

Kitty's eyes shifted wildly from side to side. He chuckled as she pulled on her wrists. "Slow and easy," he said. "Contrary to what you must be thinking, slow is often better." He maintained the same steady pace along her engorged clit and listened intently to Kitty's panting. Her eyes rounded, telling him she was very close. He glanced down at her clit. "Damn, I didn't think she could get any larger." Kitty's vagina squeezed his cock tight.

He didn't move except for the rhythmic motion of finger and thumb. "Almost, girl. Come for me."

"Oh fucking yes! I'm coming. I'm lost."

Immediately, Jared left her clitoris, reared back and began pumping in and out of her pussy, seeking his own release. His howls mingled with hers as he spurted repeatedly. His thighs jerked haphazardly, as if there was more.

Gasping for air, he slid up Kitty's perspiring body. She wrapped her legs around his butt. "Kiss me, you bastard," she said at last.

He started with the corner of her mouth and worked slowly to the other corner. He eyed her cautiously. "Are you okay?"

"As okay as any girl could be who lost count of her orgasms. Jesus, that was exquisite. Do you do that thing with the clit for all your women? That was a first for me."

He chuckled against her neck. "That pleases me immensely. You do have a very responsive clit."

"Umm. If we're done congratulating each other, do you think you could untie me?"

"Of course. I'm sorry. I forgot." He untied the knots, handed her the scarf and watched her sniff the area that had encased her loins. "So maybe you did have something to offer that hasn't been tried or used?"

"Maybe I did," Kitty said with pride. He watched her brush her clitoral area and vulva gingerly. "But my clit may be off limits for a few days after that." She dangled the scarf before his eyes, letting one end drift down to his limp cock. "I knew this gift would be useful. I hope you're looking forward to me using it on you as much as I am."

"But not tonight?" He swallowed.

She shook her head. "I want my reservoir full

when I come after you with this. Right now I'm completely drained." She yawned. "I don't know about you—I'm about ready to fall asleep. Can we cuddle?"

"I wouldn't want to displease the lady," Jared said, wrapping his arms around Kitty and tugging her close. By the time he kissed her forehead she was asleep.

CHAPTER SIX

Stretching, Kitty yawned and groaned at muscles still complaining from the previous night's overuse. She hadn't realized how taut she must've held her body when she and Jared played with the silk scarf. She dipped her hand under the sheet to say good morning to her still chafed vulva. Closing her eyes, she hated to admit it, but a bare pussy offered no protection from the kind of friction it had been subjected to so recently.

At least she'd allayed her fears that Jared might be too much of a gentleman. He'd almost taken a perverse delight in prolonging her orgasm. And he'd known with her wrists tied to the bedposts, she was entirely at his mercy. She patted her pussy and nearly purred. He'd shown very little mercy. But then she wouldn't be showing him any when she had *him* tied down.

She tossed an arm to the side to check on her handsome tormentor. Nothing. Her eyes popped wide open. "What the…"

She jerked to a sitting position and checked the alarm clock. Heaving a sigh, she tossed her head from side to side. She never slept this late, even on a Sunday morning.

She sniffed the air. Damn, was that coffee? She slipped off the bed and hoped her legs could still work. To her surprise, they did. Quickly, she made a stop in the bathroom and then put on a robe and headed out of the bedroom.

As she made her way down the stairs, the coffee aroma became pleasantly pungent. Kitty crossed the dining room to the kitchen and started to say good morning when she realized Jared wasn't in the kitchen, either.

She scowled. The hairs on the back of her neck rose and she peeked down at her bare toes sticking out from beneath the robe. She tried not to think. She tried to ignore the sense of things not being right. Where the hell was he?

She turned to the coffeemaker and gasped. There next to it was note. Didn't he even have the balls to tell her in person he was dumping her?

Picking up the note, Kitty tried to focus on the words shaking before her eyes.

> *Hi Kitty,*
>
> *Sorry, but I have to be in London ASAP. Things have gone to hell there with one of my suppliers. You were sleeping so soundly I didn't want to wake you.*
>
> *Trust that wasn't too much for you last night. I'll never forget that image or your squeals.*
>
> *Hope the coffee isn't too strong. See ya.*
> *JJ*

"What the fuck?" Kitty read over the words

once more before balling up the paper and tossing it in the trash.

"Hope the coffee isn't too strong." Weren't those lovely words for a final parting?

The guy had no flair with goodbyes.

Kitty tried not to sniffle. She swiped the back of her fists across her eyes. "The bastard." She'd just begun to look forward to an affair that might last more than a week or two. She'd even wondered what his ranch looked like.

And she'd looked forward to knocking that devilish smirk off his face when she had him tied up so she could play with whatever she wanted to bring him to an excruciatingly slow climax. She owed him that.

She poured a cup of coffee and plopped down on a kitchen chair. She took a sip and shook her head. It was strong. She took another sip. But not too strong.

Would she ever see Jared Jacobs again? Highly unlikely. But if she did, there would be hell to pay. She'd exact more than a pound of flesh.

Would he call? She shrugged. Did she even want him to call?

She'd learned the best way to get over a man was to take on another one. There were plenty for her to choose from.

She sighed and studied her coffee cup through blurry eyes. She wasn't ready for another man yet. Jared was probably on a plane. Given the urgency of his departure, it might take a day or two for him to get back to her.

She hated waiting. She'd give him a week. She tilted her head to the side. Well, most of a week. If she hadn't heard from him by the weekend, then she was going back on the prowl.

- o -

Exhausted by the end of Friday and a grueling week, Jared stretched out on the bed in his London hotel. It had taken longer to appease the copper supplier than he'd expected. One damn problem with commodities was keeping all the middle people happy.

He had an early morning flight to Amsterdam. Hopefully, Maya Narong wouldn't be so problematic. He smiled ruefully. The woman of Dutch-Thai descent had been much more pleasurable than problematic over the decade or so he'd known her. That she was a vice president of one the major European banks he dealt with was also handy.

She'd be a change from Kitty Paige — more demure, less demanding.

Kitty.

He hadn't counted on Kitty worming her way into his thoughts these last several days, but she had. He groaned. He bet she had really put her claws out when she read the note he'd left.

He hadn't planned on leaving that abruptly, but maybe it was for the better. He'd purposely kept his note vague because he didn't know what to do with his vision in yellow. She'd far surpassed his expectations, but that didn't mean he needed more of her.

Jared did his best to ignore his growing arousal. Maybe it was best to let it be. Probably neither of them was looking for anything long term. His trip to London and Europe offered a natural breaking off point.

Still, he felt a little guilty for not saying he'd call or how much he'd enjoyed their brief time together.

He glanced at his cell phone on the nightstand. He could still call her. What was holding him back?

He rolled over, facing away from the phone. She'd made no effort to call his cell, either. Maybe she'd been looking for an easy way out, too.

So how many men had she invited to her bed since he left? Involuntarily, he ground his teeth. Why should the answer to that question bother him at all?

- o -

Kitty beamed proudly at Rocketman, who was breathing hard in the winner's circle. Lawrence, Rebecca and Jared were right—there weren't many things more thrilling than getting your picture taken with your winning horse.

Ron Woods grabbed her hand and clutched it

tightly. She smiled at him and looked back at the cameraman. The construction foreman had readily agreed to be her date for the day — and, they both knew, for the night. They'd hooked up a couple times before and he'd been fun. Eight years her junior, he was safe; she knew neither one of them harbored any intentions other than some good clean fun.

And she was ready for some fun. *He* hadn't called once. *He* was gone. She was determined to get on with her life. Once she heard the camera snap, she leaned over and kissed Ron's cheek.

As they exited the winner's circle, Rebecca drew her aside. "Do what you must, girl," the older woman said, "but I can't believe your Clark Gable mustache just up and left you."

"Well, he did," Kitty snorted. "That's life."

"He struck me as a man with more common sense than that. You two looked good together." Rebecca winked. "Real good."

"And Ron and I don't?"

"I didn't say that." Rebecca shrugged and then laughed. "I believe your horseman has more potential, but you run along and enjoy your construction guy. And I'll wager you haven't seen the last of Jared Jacobs."

Kitty ignored the slight shiver at the base of her spine. "Potential doesn't do a damn thing for me. And I'll accept that wager. Let's say an expensive bottle of wine.

"You're on. If he's not back on the scene within

a month, I'll present you with the best I can afford."

Rebecca sounded way too confident. Smiling, Kitty said, "I may even share a glass with you and Lawrence."

"You seem distracted tonight."

Kitty swallowed and opened her eyes to stare up at Ron, hovering over her. She clenched her vagina around his cock and his smile was instantaneous. It wasn't fair to him to let herself be distracted by some bastard thousands of miles away. "Sorry. I must still be reliving that race Rocketman ran. Why don't you come in me?" She wrapped her legs around his butt.

"If you want," he said, shifting his weight to his knees and slipping his large hands under her rear. He hoisted her ass off the bed and eased in and out of her.

"Oh, I want," she replied. "Hurry."

Holding her steady, he pummeled her with abandon.

She strummed her clit and saw his eyes widen. She laughed when they both came together.

When he lowered her butt to the bed, she pulled away from him and curled into a ball. Her lungs heaved for air as if she were drowning. The familiar post orgasmic glow flowed through her body, yet she couldn't shake an overwhelming sense of sadness.

She shook her head. She wasn't going to go

there. No way.

She smiled when she heard Ron searching for his clothes. One thing she really liked about the guy was he didn't want to stay the night. He often had to leave for job sites by five A.M., and his tools and trailer were at his place.

"Thanks," she said softly.

"Thank you," he replied, buttoning his shirt. "You did seem to regain focus."

"Oh, yeah. Can you come by Wednesday after work? I'll fix supper."

Ron cocked his head to the side, as if mentally checking his calendar. "That'll work."

"Can you do the track next Saturday?"

He shook his head. "Sorry. I promised a friend I'd start her porch on Saturday. I could do Sunday, if you want."

"Okay," Kitty said, sitting up and not bothering to cover up. "Drop by here late morning and we can do the day at the track."

His face lit up in a grin. "And the night?"

She patted the bed by her side. "Right here, of course. Now, run along."

"See ya," he said, heading for the door.

She frowned at his back and then at the empty space. At least he'd said those words to her directly. Mr. Sunshine had only thought of putting them on a piece of paper.

She pulled her knees up and hugged them to her chest, rested her chin on them and rocked softly. So life was returning to normal.

She grimaced. Shouldn't normal feel better than this?

- o -

Gasping for breath, his eyelids half shut, Jared watched the short-cropped dark head gliding up and down his cock. He curled his toes into the carpet of Maya's living room carpet and rocked on the balls of his feet.

He stilled when Maya squeezed her small fingers around the base of his cock. His penis cooled as soon as she lifted her pretty face to giggle at him.

"I want him to come down my throat." The corners of her mouth turned up and she gave him a coy look. "If you don't mind." She slid her hand along his length, keeping him primed.

"Go ahead," he grunted, cupping his palms over her ears. He'd pay her back later. They had plenty of time.

She cradled his balls and glanced up at him. She tapped the head of his cock against each of her nipples and then lowered her head again, arching her neck.

Mesmerized, Jared watched his cock slowly but surely disappear into Maya's hot mouth. She reached around to knead his butt, drawing him tighter to her. Jared tried to swallow and breathe through his nose. He'd never understand how such a petite woman could do this, but it was her gift.

Her moans intensified as she edged closer to her goal. And then she reached it. Her lips brushed against his loins with his cock completely engulfed in her mouth and throat. Jared remained rock solid still, letting Maya adjust to his size.

She pinched his butt and he yelped. Her muffled giggle was the only prelude to her slowly moving back up his length. The suction brought an involuntary howl from his mouth.

Her shoulders shook with laughter. She knew very well what she was doing to him. She'd probably done it a hundred times before. It was never quite clear to him which one of them enjoyed this most.

He massaged the base of her neck and shoulders. She paused and moved her head from side to side without giving up her purchase.

Then she peeked up and shook her head. She winked and sleepily corkscrewed down his cock. He entwined his fingers in her hair and she began in earnest to propel them toward her next goal. Her fingers dug into his butt, encouraging his help.

He rocked back and forth, trying to keep his eyes open to watch Maya work her magic. She soon became a blur. She had him. He rose on his toes as he began coming in spurts.

Maya never hesitated or slowed. "Oh hell," he cried out. She stayed with him, not yielding at all to his distress.

At last his spasms began to ebb. He settled back on the soles of his feet. Apparently not convinced he was finished, Maya slipped a small hand around his shaft and began to milk whatever he had left over into her mouth. He groaned loudly. He wanted to pull her off, but knew she enjoyed feeling him soften in her mouth.

When his legs threatened to give out, Maya dropped his shaft from her mouth and held it gingerly in her hand. She eyed his now-limp cock and giggled. "The mighty do fall," she murmured, kissing its tip and rubbing its crown across her cheeks.

He helped her to her feet and hugged her tight. "You're too much," he groaned.

She smiled and then nipped at his pecs. "I loved that. You are a very virile man, Jared Jacobs. After three nights of loving, you still give me what I need." She placed her small hand around his. "Come, my friend. My bed is waiting. I think your tongue would be a nice gift."

Minutes later, Jared curled his tongue as Maya steadily rode it, her knees placed on either side of his head. He encouraged her with his hands curved around her bottom. He knew she was tugging on her nipples with one hand while her other was busy just above his nose, strumming her clit.

"What a ride," she squealed. Her thighs squeezed his head like a fleshy vise. "Don't move," she panted. "I'm coming."

He tried not to laugh but held his tongue steady, letting her use it as she needed. And then her juices began to ebb over his tongue. She jerked and moaned softly. She released and he had to swallow or drown.

She didn't complain as he began lapping at her pussy. He couldn't catch her entire flow. She spilled out of his mouth and down his chin.

He held her, waiting for her to regain her equilibrium. Her butt cheeks shuddered as she backed away and slid down his chest.

She grinned broadly. "You missed some." Maya flicked out her tongue and cleaned his chin of her juices. Finished, she kissed him full on the mouth and then nestled against him.

He cuddled her and kissed her cheek. "Ah, Kitty," he murmured. "You are incredible."

Maya propped herself up on an elbow and gave him a crooked grin. "So who's Kitty?"

"Kitty?" Jared froze. "I didn't!"

Maya nodded slowly. "You did." She slanted a finger across his lips. "It's okay. We both have many lovers."

"But I never..." He still couldn't believe he'd called out Kitty's name. He prided himself on being so careful with his women never to let one lover intrude upon another. *Son of a bitch.*

"You'd better tell me about her, or you're going to bust a gut."

"I'm sorry," he began. "I'll leave now, if you

want."

Looking perturbed, Maya said quickly, "I don't want you to leave. I want to hear about this Kitty lover." Maya grinned softly. "She must really have her claws in you."

He shrugged. Were all women as persistent as Maya and Kitty? They'd probably like each other. "I haven't known her long. She lives in Chicago. She's into real estate and into race horses." That he added race horses surprised him. After all, that was a recent interest for her.

"Ah," Maya said, "she shares your passion. Horses are much too big for me to take a liking to. But there must be more to her than that. You've seemed distracted this entire week. I thought it was work." She smirked. "But now I know it was a woman. Did she do you wrong?"

He shook his head.

"Did you do her wrong?" She peered at him down her tiny nose.

He sighed. "She might think so."

"You don't know for sure?"

"We haven't talked since I left Chicago."

"I see. You have unfinished business in Chicago."

He closed his eyes. "Maybe."

She pecked at his lips and he opened his eyes to see her smiling down at him.

"You may be able to fool yourself for a while, but you can't fool me. You do have unfinished business." She shook her head. "I never thought

I'd see the day when Jared Jacobs became a marked man."

Maya trailed her lips down his neck and nibbled on his throat. She glanced back up at him. "Someday I'd like to meet this Kitty of yours. She must be quite the woman. Does she know you love her?"

"I don't," he snapped.

"So you say. I hope you won't be offended if I don't believe you." She shifted lower, nipping at his shoulders. His cock sprang to life as she began rubbing her crotch against it.

He tilted his head to the side. "You're not upset? This week?"

She shook her head. "Of course not. We both needed some loving. We've always done well together without strings. This is no different."

Maya tucked a hand between them to bring his stiff shaft to her pussy. She smiled and gasped as she bore down, taking him into her tight sleeve.

"Kitty may have her claws in you, but she hasn't claimed you completely. Not yet." She placed her palms on his chest and pushed up to a sitting position. "You are mine tonight." She levered up his shaft and back down. "Unless you object."

He growled and reached for her breasts. "You and Kitty probably have more in common than I want to admit."

She gyrated from side to side and up and down. Her nipples became hard pinpoints. Her darker skin seemed such a contrast to Kitty's ivory flesh.

Maya stopped rising and falling to grind against his loins. "She and I share a cock, at least for now." Maya narrowed her eyes. "But now I don't want to hear her name again tonight." She flashed an eyebrow. "If I do, I may have to get my whips out. Agreed?"

He chuckled softly, not sure she was joking. "Agreed." He curled his fingers around her hips to help her ride both of them into oblivion.

Sitting in a window seat in first class, Jared ignored everything going on around him. With his eyes closed to ward off any intrusion from flight attendants, he plotted and re-plotted his strategy for Kitty Paige.

Would she even talk to him after he'd left so abruptly? He'd make her. He shifted his eyes from side to side—he couldn't make that damn woman do a thing.

He'd have to resort to romance. He smiled. Wasn't that what he'd done after she left him hanging in Seattle? The roses. The scarf.

And she'd responded. He chuckled softly, remembering the yellow thong and yellow vibrator.

She'd figure out some way to make him grovel, and he had that coming to him. He'd behaved like an idiot. Maya was right; he'd probably inflated his business crisis to get out of Chicago before he could sink into the quicksand of Kitty's making. He sighed. They were both responsible, but did she have any idea how she'd so completely captured his imagination?

From Chicago to London to Amsterdam he'd been troubled by his reaction to Kitty. Why did it take another woman to name that trouble? *Love!*

He didn't want to be in love. He nearly gagged, and then he felt like soaring. Love was the last thing he'd wanted when he first sent the roses. He took a deep breath and blew air through his lips. Love was what he got.

He thought of Maya's goodbye and well wishes and smiled. He'd miss her. She'd always made it clear they had only what they shared from moment to moment. She seldom took male lovers to her bed, saying she found females lovers to be more sensitive and less complicated. Fortunately, she'd always made an exception for him. And she knew if he got what he wanted from Kitty, their sexual friendship would end—but their non-sexual friendship and business relationship would survive. They shared far too much for that not to happen.

Jared cracked his eyes open to check his watch and then quickly closed them. With luck, they'd land at O'Hare early in the evening. Should he simply knock on her door and surprise her?

He pursed his lips. That might be too dangerous. He could blow their entire future with the wrong step. He didn't like calling her first to

give warning, but that did seem to have the least amount of risk.

Advanced knowledge would give her a chance to collect herself. Clearly, they had things to talk about. He didn't think she'd simply invite him to her bed.

He smiled. She did have a very large comfortable bed. He'd see if he could find some yellow roses at the airport.

Jared sighed deeply. With a plan settled, he allowed himself to drift off.

- o -

"Damn," Kitty grunted. "Wait a minute," she said to Ron, who had just begun to take her to that next plateau on the way to another glorious orgasm.

He stopped immediately.

"Don't go away," she said, locking a leg around his butt to keep him in place. "I've got to check caller I.D. I've got a huge sale hanging in the balance. If it's the buyer's realtor, I'm going to have to take the call."

"No problem," Ron said, rising off her chest to kneel. He wiggled his cock in her, as if to assure her he wasn't about to shrivel up.

Kitty grabbed her cell from the nightstand. At first the cell phone number didn't register in her foggy brain, and then it did. "Oh my God," she said, ignoring Ron's questioning look.

She pushed a button and put the phone to her ear. "This better be good. Where the hell are you?"

"At O'Hare. I just got back."

"Oh." His voice had cracked, as if he wasn't quite sure what to say next. She saw no need to bail him out. She waited, flexing her hips slightly against Ron.

"Can I come over? I'd like to see you. I need to talk with you."

"It's getting late. You didn't seem to have much to say when you left two weeks ago. Can't it wait till morning?"

"I'd really like to talk with you tonight." He paused.

She heard his sigh over the phone.

"I'd really like to start where we left off. I've done a lot of thinking these past two weeks."

"So you want to come over and pick up from where we left off. When we were still talking."

"Yes. I can make it up to you — but I need to see you."

"Okay." Kitty pursed her lips and then broke into a smile. "We'll start where we left off. I'll have the downstairs open. When you get here, let yourself in, lock the door and come up to my bedroom. I'll be waiting for you. My pussy is already wet," she purred. "You might be thinking about that, and also about how I might exact a little payback from you. Bye," she said abruptly, not wanting to prolong their discussion about the night's activities.

116

She giggled when she looked back at Ron, who was shaking his head.

"You can be a very nasty girl, Kitty Paige."

"Don't you know it?"

"Do you want me to leave?"

She tipped her pelvis and teased him subtly. "Of course not. You remember our night with Tom?"

Smirking, Ron flexed in and out of her pussy. "Do you think I'll ever forget that night?"

"I hope not." She placed her hands on his chest. "Now why don't you pull out and save yourself until later? I have to go down and unlock the door."

Ron rolled over onto his back with his full cock jutting toward the ceiling. Rising to her knees, Kitty squeezed his cock and kissed its tip. "Sorry, guy. You'll get yours yet tonight, I promise."

She crawled off the bed and stretched to her full height. She smiled down at Ron. "I've suddenly become quite famished—for a man-sandwich. I'll be right back. Don't go anywhere."

She didn't bother with a wrap as she left the bedroom to go down and unlock the main door. Her nipples couldn't pebble more than they already had.

So he wanted back in her life. Had he decided he'd left prematurely? Did he really think she'd simply welcome him back with open arms?

She smirked. Actually, that was her plan. He might be a little surprised by that gesture, but he'd probably be even more surprised to discover she already had a cock buried in her ass.

She hoped Jared wouldn't be shy meeting a stranger. Would he storm out of her bedroom?

If he did, she didn't give a damn. If he wanted back, she'd have him on her terms or not at all.

She winced as she climbed the stairs. She hadn't realized she'd allowed him to hurt her so. Why was she even toying with him?

Because she was angry, hurt and hot as hell. She missed his damn smirk, his bantering, and playing with his mustache. And his damn cock.

But it was payback time. She had no idea how long it might take for them to be even again. Would he play her game?

She chewed on her bottom lip and paused at the top of the stairs. Kitty glanced back at the unlocked door. She sure hoped he would. The opportunity for two cocks didn't happen every week.

CHAPTER SEVEN

Softly, Jared closed Kitty's entryway door behind him. He set his luggage down and called out, "I'm here."

"Hurry up. I'm waiting."

The strained sound of her voice made him smile—maybe she was as eager to see him as he was to see her.

He bounded up the stairs two at a time and slowed as he saw the soft light of the open bedroom doorway. He wet his lips, took a deep breath and entered.

"Jesus H. Christ." The woman he loved lay on her back atop another man's broad chest, with her arms and legs akimbo, baiting him and showing clearly that the man's cock was buried to the hilt in her ass.

"Welcome back, lover," Kitty purred, beckoning him with her fingers. "I've saved a special place for you." She dipped a hand to her pussy, as if he might have any doubts. "Oh, forgive me for the oversight. Jared, this is Ron. Ron, this is Jared. I doubt if last names will be necessary."

The young man flashed him a brief nod and Jared nodded automatically. He took a half step backward.

"If you walk out on me again, Jared, don't bother coming back or calling. This is what I want. If you're not man enough to play with me, then go fuck yourself."

He shook his head. "Didn't take you long to come up with a replacement."

"I waited a week. Did you wait that long?"

"Barely," he admitted. "Is this…" he waved his hand at her and the stranger, "supposed to shock me out of your life?"

She grinned and flexed her hips a little, sliding along the man's cock. "You tell me."

He reached for his belt and smiled when her eyes rounded. He pulled the belt out of its loops. "I should use this on you."

"But you won't," she said confidently.

"How can you be so sure?" he said, pushing his boots off and then his pants and shorts. His cock sprang forward as if it had sniffed its favorite home.

"You might want to do a lot of things to me, but you don't have a mean bone in your body. Now why don't you bring that big fellow over her so I can get him wet?"

Was he too hung up on her to deny her? Or had he merely become jaded? He walked to the bed and watched her lick his length while he undid the buttons on his shirt and tossed it aside.

She held him with both hands and turned her head away from him. "Ron, why don't you use a little more lube? We're just about ready."

120

Jared tried not to look too closely, but he saw enough to know that Ron, the ass man, was well hung. He hadn't expected any less from Kitty. It was going to be a tight squeeze.

"You're serious about this?"

"Of course I'm serious." She arched an eyebrow. "I've been telling Ron ever since you called how much I'm hungry for a man sandwich." She pulled back and narrowed her eyes. "I trust you can deliver."

Jared tipped back his head and laughed. "Will you ever stop trying to challenge me? If our friend can do his part, and it looks like he can, we'll get you well fucked."

He peered down at the curious gray eyes next to Kitty. "Ron, I hope you're not in a hurry. I want this woman begging before we completely satisfy her hunger. Agreed?"

"Absolutely," Ron said. "I like a man who takes time with a woman."

"Good. Maybe I'll buy you a beer when we're finished here."

Jared got on the bed and chuckled when he caught sight of Kitty's jaw dropping. Had she really thought she could get rid of him so easily? He'd already told her once she'd only be rid of him when *he* agreed. He grinned to himself. He couldn't imagine anything she could do or say that was going scare him off.

He knelt between their legs and scooted forward. He dropped a kiss on her gaping pussy,

121

and raised his head to wink at her. "Doesn't look like you need much more foreplay."

- o -

Kitty cast a wary look at Jared. He seemed to be enjoying himself too much. She knew he'd been dumbfounded when he entered her room, but he'd clearly recovered and was trying to retake control.

She wet her lips as he rubbed his cock up and down her vulva. This was what she wanted, but they weren't going to make her beg.

She tried not to wince when she felt the tip of his cock enter her portal. Ron, for his part, held perfectly still, letting Jared find his way. She swallowed as her vagina stretched trying to find room for this most recent intruder.

Jared paused.

Kitty read concern in his eyes. At least, that was what she thought she saw. It was what she hoped she saw.

"You're tight with one cock. Expand for me."

"I'm trying, damn it. Give me a moment to adjust." She clenched her teeth. "More." She smiled as she felt more of him enter.

He paused. "You don't have to take all of him."

"The hell I don't." She thrust her pelvis, careful not to dislodge Ron. She took more of Jared and grinned broadly. She had indeed taken all of him—all of *them*, really.

"You will." His gaze bore into her. Ron didn't assist him in any way. Jared's hands were at her sides as he leaned forward and arched upward, deepening his penetration.

His cock and her pussy were in some sort of tug of war. Her eyes widened; she knew what he was searching for. "Oh hell," she cried out, rolling her eyes to the back of her head. "I'm coming again. Jesus, stop. I'm coming."

Relentlessly, he pounded her G spot. She saw stars. She blinked her eyes open.

"Say it," he demanded. "Beg me to stop."

She squealed. He wasn't going to stop. She was one big orgasm. She giggled. He was fucking an orgasm. She'd gotten what she wanted. She held on. She raised a hand to slap him, but it fell to the bed.

He was endless energy running on adrenalin. "That's it," she called out. "Stop. I beg you, stop."

He stopped immediately.

Her eyes sprang wide open as another orgasm teetered. "Once more," she panted.

His laughter filled her ears. His smiled warmed her as he drove into her again. "That's it," she said trying to breathe through her open mouth. "That's it."

This time he pulled out of her and neither man tried to stop her when she slid away from them and curled into a ball. Shudders wracked her body. They darted from her pussy and from her asshole but they spread throughout. Not a single

125

cell, not a single pore was left out. "What a fucking night," she murmured to no one in particular. She wept tears of pleasure and joy.

She must've drifted, because when she stirred she was alone on the bed. Groggy, she rose to a sitting position to see Jared in a brown robe sitting in the cushion chair opposite the bed. Ron's clothes were missing. He had an early morning coming up.

She settled back against the pillow, uncertain how the remainder of her morning would go, but she'd certainly had a tremendous night.

She wrinkled her nose and widened her eyes. "Do I smell coffee?"

"I took the liberty to make some. Hope you don't mind."

"Of course not. At least this time you stayed around to share it." She moved back to a sitting position as he carried a steaming coffee mug to her. "I suppose you want to talk?"

His mouth crinkled into a smile. "Unless you have any other guys, or women, or any other kinky need to take care of first."

"No," she yawned and covered her mouth. "I can't think of anything at the moment. You're looking at a very exhausted but very satisfied woman. And if you were serious about your question, I'm not into women. I tried it couple times in my twenties. Nothing wrong with it, just wasn't my thing." She sipped her coffee. She yawned again and saw his white shirt on the floor next to his chair. "Would you toss me your shirt? I'm a little chilled."

He tossed it to her without getting out of the chair. She poked her arms into the sleeves and buttoned the bottom two buttons. She knew she seldom looked sexier than when wearing a man's shirt. And she definitely wanted to look and feel sexy. "So what do you want to talk about?"

"How are you?" he asked, with a twitch in his cheek. "Sore? Can you move?"

She flashed an eyebrow and ran a hand over her abs. "Damn, you were really cranking into me."

He coughed. "Yeah, well I kind of lost control there for a bit."

"Really?" She brightened. "I like that. So do I bring the best and the worst out of you?"

"You could say that."

Jared looked like a sphinx sitting across from her. His legs, crossed at the ankles, belied an alertness she'd come to recognize as a sign he was about to surprise her. Maybe her best maneuver was to take the initiative. "You've met Ron. So tell me about the woman you were with in London."

Jared remained passive. "It was in Amsterdam. I've known Maya for years."

"It wasn't your first time."

"Hardly," he snorted. "Maya is part Dutch and part Thai. She's the person who first introduced me to the Thai silk scarf and how one might use

127

it."

"That was fun," Kitty purred. "So did you talk to her about me?"

"Not on purpose."

Kitty frowned. She watched his fingers curl into fists and then relax.

"It's never happened to me before." He squared his shoulders and stared hard at her. "I called her *Kitty* in the afterglow of lovemaking."

Kitty jerked to a sitting position. "Really?" She wet her lips as he slowly nodded. "Wow." She grinned broadly and pounded the mattress with her feet. "I can't tell you what that does for a girl's ego."

"Yeah, well maybe not quite so much for the girl you're with at the time. I felt like a jerk."

"Poor boy," Kitty cooed, hardly believing what he was saying. But his nonverbal discomfort gave her no reason to doubt him. So he hadn't forgotten her, even with another woman. She felt a little shiver run up her spine—thrill? Or fear? She couldn't tell. "What about Maya? How did she respond?"

"Oh, Maya is a gracious woman. She laughed it off as something that happens."

"She wasn't jealous? Doesn't she want you for herself?" Kitty flinched, not sure where that last question had come from.

"No, to both questions. If and when Maya wants to take on a permanent partner, it'll probably be a woman." His cheeks colored a little.

"I'm sort of an exception for Maya."

Kitty stretched back out against the pillows and turned on her side to face him. She lifted her top leg and rested its foot on the knee of her lower leg, framing her pussy for him. "You do have your exceptional moments. So this Maya didn't have any problems fucking you even after you called her Kitty."

Jared's lips thinned and his gaze worked slowly up her body from her toes to her smile. "Of course not. If anything, my faux pas energized her. Maya doesn't think we'll get back together again in that way."

"Really?" She lowered her leg and drew her knees to her chest. "Why not?" She wasn't at all sure she wanted to know, but she had to ask.

"Maya believes you have your claws in me and won't let me go."

"Me? Not true." She smiled as best she could, fighting a stomach that churned like a cement mixer. She held up her hands and waved her fingernails at him. "I know I've scratched your back pretty good, but I don't believe I drew blood. Does she think she's a soothsayer? I don't do it on purpose. I never know what I'm going to do when I'm hanging on that thin edge."

"So maybe I bring the best and worst out of you, too."

"Hmm. Perhaps. I'm not sure if that's good or bad."

"But you haven't had enough of me?"

129

She breathed through her nose, not trusting herself to open her mouth. He seemed determined to push them onto shaky ground. She shook her head cautiously.

"Good." He smiled warmly. "That's at least a start."

A start. *A start of what*, she wanted to ask, but she held her tongue. Jared remained silent so long she had to say something. "So you like this Maya."

"That should be obvious."

"And you trust her."

"Sure." Jared seemed quite puzzled by her line of questioning.

"She does sound intriguing. Do you think I'll ever meet her?"

"Probably not." A corner of his mouth turned up. "That's likely for the best."

"Why's that?"

"The two of you would probably get involved in a war of wills. When Maya finds a woman she likes, she seldom backs off until she has her in bed. I've seen her art of seduction several times."

Kitty squinted and pursed her lips. "You think Maya would like me," she swallowed, " — want me?"

"Absolutely. Maya has excellent taste when it comes to women."

"I see. So does that mean you have excellent taste in women?"

"Exactly. And I'm looking at the most tasty woman I've ever known."

"Cripes." Kitty trembled slightly. His words jarred her. "I don't think I want to meet your Maya woman. I have my hands full with you. Do you think you can come over here and hold me?"

"I'd be happy to." Jared stood. "You're not trying to cut off this conversation with sex, are you?"

"No," she murmured, sliding into his welcoming arms as he settled beside her. "My pussy and ass are going to be off limits for a few more hours." She smirked. "Of course that does leave my mouth available."

He shook his head. "I believe my guy could stand a rest for a few hours, too." He cocked his head. "No regrets about last night?"

She giggled and kissed his mouth softly. "If you're looking for an apology, you won't get it. I'm a girl who likes two cocks now and then. Do you have regrets?"

He shook his head. "Nope. It galls me a little to have to share you at all. But I doubt even I could ever get you that totally fucked. And it was nice that Ron couldn't hang around long afterward."

"So did you guys really go downstairs while I slept and have a beer?"

He nodded.

She scowled. "You didn't scare Ron off did you? He's one of my best construction guys. You should see him with a nail gun. He can hang more wall board in an hour than any three guys."

Jared shook his head. "I wanted to tell him to

never get within a hundred feet of you again, but I didn't. I don't own you, Kitty, and I never want to."

"So you'd do a repeat performance." She arched an eyebrow. "I won't scare you off if I desire two cocks?"

Jared closed his eyes and gripped her rear with his large hand and hugged her tight.

She was nearly overcome with the warmth pouring from this man. When had he developed such an emotional need for her? Damn. Damn. Damn. How long could she afford to stay involved with him?

His lips kissed their way across her forehead and then he leaned back and stared softly at her. "You're not going to scare me off. When are you going to start believing that?"

Her breath caught somewhere in her windpipe. "You didn't really answer my question."

"I don't suppose a cock and a vibrator are the same as two cocks."

She giggled and smoothed his mustache with an index finger. "It's not the same."

"I trust you won't need a steady diet of two cocks."

"That would take the fun out of it. And I do have to get up and go to work most days."

He planted a kiss on the tip of her nose. "So are we working out the ground rules here for some sort of relationship?"

"It does have that feel about it." She kissed the

corner of his mouth and dragged her teeth on his mustache. "As long as you don't expect too much from me. I don't have much experience with relationships that last more than a month." She narrowed her eyes. "And Ron doesn't count. We pick each other up when the other is down, but we don't see ourselves as involved in anything other than that. We're good friends and have been for years."

"To answer some of your questions, I don't have a timeframe in mind. I want to get to know you better — much better." He leaned away and shook his head playfully. "Not sex. I want to get to know you as a person, as a woman."

"And."

"I enjoy being with you. I'd love you to come out and see my ranch. From what I've seen, you could use a vacation."

"Maybe." She was curious to know how Jared lived. She'd convinced herself it was only curiosity. And she never did believe in that old adage, *curiosity kills the cat.*

"As to your other question," Jared continued, "I'll make a bargain with you. I'll share you with another cock — a healthy cock — from time to time, if there are no other cocks when I'm not around."

She smiled broadly. "You do drive a hard bargain." She slipped a hand inside his robe and dragged a fingernail over his pecs. "And what about other women?"

"I thought you weren't into women," he teased.

She scratched his chest until he yelped. "You know that's not what I meant. If I can't have other cocks, you can't have other pussies. Do you have a problem with that?"

"Nope." He covered her hand with his. She guessed they both could feel his heart pumping. "I was hoping you might come around to my point of view."

"Until you tire of me, or I tire of you," she said before covering his mouth with hers.

"That's good enough for me. Stay put."

She watched him move off the bed and reach into his trousers. Her body cooled quickly without his warmth. She arched an eyebrow when he handed her a small package.

"Something I picked up in Amsterdam hoping we might work out some sort of agreeable arrangement," he tilted his head, "at least for the short run."

She did her best to ignore any implication he might intend and dug into the small package—a yellow diamond belly ring. "This is perfect," she squealed. "I've been thinking about getting another belly ring for a while now. This is absolutely perfect." She pulled up the tails of his white shirt that she still wore and held the diamond over her turquoise ring. "I'll put it in later. So do you think this is enough yellow to make me that vision in yellow you keep teasing me about?"

He shook his head. "It helps." He ran his

fingers through her tresses. "Your straw blond hair and your broad smile is enough for that."

"Damn," she said, pulling his head to her shoulder. "You can be the most romantic guy sometimes." She ran her trembling fingers through his hair. "You don't know how scary that can be for me."

"I'm beginning to," he said softly against her shoulder. "Keep talking to me. I don't want to scare you too much, too quickly."

She heaved as he sighed and nuzzled her ear. "I think right now the best thing we can do is stop talking." She hugged him tighter still. "But I do love the yellow diamond. Did Maya help you pick it out?"

"Yes. She's rooting for us."

"Damn. Ssh," She whispered. "I don't want to talk any more. Just hold me, please."

Jared said nothing but cuddled her close.

Why did she feel like she'd just taken a huge, irrevocable step, like the Fool on the card in one of her Tarot decks? She jerked her eyes wide open. Jared was already asleep. She hadn't thought about or used her Tarot cards in years. She snuggled closer to her male heat source. Maybe it was time to check back in with that mystical side of her she so often wanted to deny.

- o -

Feigning sleep, Jared hummed a soft tune in his

head. He'd gotten more of a commitment out of Kitty than he'd expected. There was no timeframe. But they had agreed to an exclusive relationship — well, sort of. At least he wasn't going to have to worry about her taking on all the males in Chicago without him present. And he did trust her, and he knew if she absolutely wanted out, she'd tell him. That was about all he could hope for, for now.

He'd take his time with her. She could be skittish as a young filly.

He thought of the spectacular grin on her face when she'd spied the diamond belly ring. He smiled — he couldn't have made a better selection. Again, he was thankful for Maya's assistance.

Ah, Maya. He would miss holding the petite woman in his arms, but he'd never let his Kitty go without a real fight.

He wondered if Kitty knew there were cases in the animal world where a lioness sank her claws so deeply into its prey it couldn't let go.

CHAPTER EIGHT

After rearranging his stock portfolio, Jared hit the exit button and snapped his laptop shut. He glanced around the spare bedroom Kitty had set him up in for a temporary office. Even he was surprised by how smoothly the last several days had gone since his return from Amsterdam. With the Chicago Mercantile Exchange located in the city, he had plenty to do and had taken the time to renew some long dormant contacts. Many traders considered Chicago to be the hub of the commodities world. He'd traveled enough to know that might not be exactly true, but it was close enough.

Most importantly, his love life had smoothed out. Kitty would go on guard if he pushed her too hard, but she didn't seem intent on trying to scare him off. That was progress.

She was as difficult to satisfy in bed as usual, but she seemed to have found a reservoir of patience he hadn't noticed before he'd gone to London. He didn't count on that lasting.

She really did seem pleased with the yellow diamond. She'd put it in place later the morning he'd given it to her, and she hadn't replaced it yet. He loved the way it sparkled as she thrashed beneath him.

He chuckled. She'd accepted that diamond without pause. How long could he wait before giving her the diamond he really wanted her to wear?

He shook his head. "Easy," he muttered. It might take months to wear her down that much—even years. In time, he'd wear her down—he pulled on his mustache—with romance and simply with being around. She'd wake up some morning and know she didn't want to spend another day without him, and then he'd strike. She might fight him, but he would persevere. He'd been a marathon runner in college. Those races paled compared to the one he was now running.

Did she know he was racing for her heart? He delighted in her body, but he wouldn't be satisfied until he'd claimed her heart and had given his to her.

The key to the race was reading her non-verbals—not necessarily what she said, but how she reacted. Kitty was an extremely kinetic woman. Maybe that explained her wildness in bed. Unlike him, she had a difficult time being passive. She'd tilt her chin lower and give him a very pensive if not frightened look when he asked for too much emotion from her or when he didn't monitor his own.

She wanted him, but she hadn't yet decided she wanted or needed all of him. He flexed his shoulders and winced at the sudden pain. Did she know she'd drawn blood the night before when she clawed his back as he spilled into her?

What would Maya make of that?

Jared checked his watch. Kitty would be back in an hour and a half. He still had time to shower and then make the light supper he'd promised to have ready when she got home.

He hadn't felt this domestic in years, if ever. It would be good to head back to the track tomorrow. He'd begun to miss the smell of horses badly.

He sighed. Soon he'd have to head back to his ranch. It wasn't that he was needed to run it, he just missed the place. Was Kitty too big-city to be comfortable on a small working ranch?

"Damn," he muttered, heading toward the shower. That question was one he hadn't wanted to seriously consider. He'd hate like hell to give up his ranch, but then he was getting ahead of himself.

He brightened and laughed aloud. Maybe he'd treat her to three cocks if she agreed to move to the ranch.

- o -

"Thanks for the bottle of wine you sent over," Rebecca said to Kitty as they stopped to buy hot dogs and drinks before returning to their box to join the men.

Kitty smiled at her friend as she listened to her over the din of the Arlington Park racing crowd.

139

Apparently, they'd missed the fourth race. "I'm glad you liked it. I guess there is no such thing as a sure bet."

The older woman smiled easily. "I knew I was making a sure bet. Still, it was nice to win. Lawrence and I found some novel ways to enjoy the wine. Of course we thought of you and Jared when we shared it."

Kitty paid for their food and they both walked over to the condiment table. "I'm pleased I'm so much of an inspiration for your love life."

"Successful marriages, I believe, require inspiration and innovation, but then you wouldn't know about that."

Kitty looked sharply at Rebecca.

"I love the outfit you have on," Rebecca said, perhaps looking for a safer conversation topic. "You look tremendous in canary yellow. And I've always loved the shirtdress style. The wide black belt works, too. And those high heeled sandals are to die for. Tell me about them."

Kitty shrugged. "I thought the thin straps made my feet look more naked than when I was barefoot." She grinned. "And I couldn't resist the four jewels from toes to ankles. I was surprised by how comfortable they are."

Rebecca winked at her when she finished spreading relish and mustard on a hot dog. "I know one thing that'd make you look even sexier."

"What?"

"When I was a teen we wore our collars up a little." She wiped her fingers on a napkin. "Like this."

Kitty stood still and let Rebecca brush her hair back to fold over her collar. Kitty walked a couple feet away until she could see her reflection in glass door. "I like," she murmured. "Thanks," she said turning back to Rebecca. "I thought it might make me look too hoody."

Rebecca flashed a smile. "Maybe too sexy. I'll be amazed if Jared can keep his hands off of you." She began putting their food on a cardboard tray. "The next time you're not wearing a dress I really want to see that yellow diamond belly ring." She cocked her head to the side and her eyes sparkled. "Do you think I'm too old to surprise Lawrence with a belly ring?"

Kitty giggled with her co-conspirator. "I hope a woman is never too old for a belly ring."

Handing Jared his hot dog and fries, Kitty grinned at the lusty expression suddenly crossing his face. Rebecca was right—the raised collar was going to make the afternoon very long for Jared. Long for her, too.

"What have you two been up to," he asked, "besides food gathering?"

"Conspiring."

"Conspiring how to make me rock hard?" he whispered in her ear as she slid in front of him to take the seat on the other side.

"Of course." She batted an eyelash. "Isn't that the point?"

"Do you know you have the sexiest damn feet?"

"Uh huh." She slapped his hand off her thigh. "You've told me before. And we have a much larger crowd today, so be a good boy—for a change—if you can."

He leaned away from her and chortled, then glanced over at the tote board. "It'd be a lot easier to be a good boy if you weren't so intent on being a naughty girl." He gave her a crooked smile and laid half the *Daily Racing Form* across her lap.

She scowled at him when she felt his fingers toying with the hem of her skirt, which had ridden half way up her thigh. "If you persist on being bad, I'll have to spank you when we get back home."

He withdrew his hand from under the newspaper and leaned over to whisper in her ear. "Is that a promise?"

She burst out laughing. "Trust me. So how did we do on the last race?"

"Your horse came in right behind mine, so we not only won the race but got the exacta."

She couldn't help herself. She quickly leaned over and whispered, "So does that mean I was riding your ass?"

He shook his head and checked out the horses across the way at the starting gate with his binoculars. "So now who is taunting?"

"So how much more do I have to do before *I've* earned a spanking?"

"Not a bit more," he said out of the corner of his mouth. "You earned that when you came back to the box with your collar at such a rakish angle."

"Do we have to stay for all the races?"

He let the binoculars hang from his neck and gave her a crooked smile. "You getting a little hot?"

She nodded.

"We can leave after the eighth. Will that be soon enough for you?"

She pouted. "It'll have to be."

"So tell me," Kitty said, "do you suppose our sitting out here on my back porch sipping brandy rather than screwing in my entryway as soon as we stepped into the house is a sign of maturity, or a cooling of our relationship?"

"I like to think we're merely banking the fire so it doesn't go out in a blazing flash." Jared brought the snifter to his lips. She watched his Adam's apple bob and knew he was teasing her. "What do you think?"

Kitty blew him a kiss. "I think you might want to know that I removed my panties when I stopped in the bathroom."

"Ah, at least I won't have to rip them off you."

"That particular item in my wardrobe has been shrinking in number since you've come into my life."

Smirking, Jared brushed the back of a hand across her cheek. "I didn't intend on impoverishing you. Perhaps you ought to consider going commando."

"Uh, uh, I come across too many weirdos in my line of work. There are occasions when even I get a little nervous showing a house to a guy, or even a couple—particularly late at night."

"I hadn't thought of that." Jared's tone had shifted from playful to sober. "Maybe you should dress more conservatively—a suit perhaps."

"Nope. I won't let others change who I am. I like dressing sexy and I like feeling sexy." She raised an eyebrow. "You might be surprised by how much easier it is for me to engage people when I'm pleased with how I look."

His lips curled up.

"Maybe you wouldn't be so surprised."

He nodded. "So in order to conserve your wardrobe, you might want to think about going commando when we're together."

She reached for his hand and laid it on her bare knee, confident he'd manage to find his way from there. Rocking slowly in the wicker rocker, she confessed, "I have been giving that some serious thought. It does seem like a reasonable compromise."

"Exactly," Jared said, pushing his chair back and settling on his knees in front of her rocker. "You save on your clothes budget and trips to the store, and I can imagine you ready for attention on the whim of a moment."

He scrunched his mouth. "So is my Kitty wanting some serious attention?" He lifted her left foot and removed the high heeled sandal.

"Absolutely," she purred, slouching lower in the wicker rocker.

She shivered when he brought her foot to his mouth and laved her instep. "Oh God," Kitty whimpered as Jared took his time, drawing one toe in his mouth only to replace it with another. When he was apparently satisfied that foot was clean, he rested the leg over the arm of the rocker and reached for the other foot.

"You are a jewel," he whispered as he undid the jeweled straps on the second sandal.

He began with the top of her foot, leaving no square inch unwashed. She arched her neck against the back of wicker chair as he suckled her toes—this time all at once. He chewed on them and chuckled at her squeals.

She hiked her dress up over her waist in case he'd forgotten his objective. She knew she must be puffy and glistening by now. She'd creamed repeatedly as he began devouring her toes.

Jared draped that leg over the other arm of the chair. She had to be about as exposed and vulnerable as she'd ever been.

"Is someone feeling left out," he teased, running the tip of his tongue between his lips.

She nodded. "Very." She inched lower.

"In due time," he said, kissing first one knee

and then the other.

She peered at him though her eyelashes when his lips left her flesh.

"Do you know your clit is already on alert?"

"Not surprising," she said, gritting her teeth.

He planted a kiss on her inner thigh. She jerked forward.

"Are you posturing for me?" His lips slid along the inside of her other thigh.

She couldn't stop the moans escaping from her lips.

"Is my Kitty calling out for her Tom?"

She sighed and arched her pelvis when at last she felt his warm breath on her vulva. She smacked her lips when he moved higher to lap at her belly ring. "Jesus."

"You do look good in diamonds. Taste good, too."

"I'm glad," she replied, squirming beneath his tongue, using every trick she could come up with to get that tongue in contact with her clit.

He brushed his lips back and forth across her lower abs, avoiding her clit. He pulled away and she gasped and then grinned as his tongue began lapping at one side of her pussy and then the other.

She felt herself purr. Maybe she *was* his kitty, and he her Tom. Had any female cat worked harder to focus her Tom's attention?

His hands feathered her thighs and the tip of his tongue at last found her crevice. She spread as wide as she could and still remain in the chair. His head moved up and down and the flat of his tongue spread her pussy lips even wider.

He left her pussy to thoroughly explore the ridge between it and her anus. She hugged her breasts together, loving his attention but needing more. She wasn't going to be responsible for what she did if he stayed at this pace. With considerable effort, she resisted reaching for her clit.

His furled tongue widened her portal. "Thank God," she moaned, banging her heels against the wicker.

She thrilled when a long finger probed her channel and then nearly wept when it pulled out. Then a finger tapped at her back entrance and she knew Jared wasn't about to leave anything unexplored. "Oh, yeah." She let out a sigh, trying to be patient. Her man might seem intent on being deliberate, but she no longer questioned the merit of waiting.

She'd lost track of time, but he must've been eating her for half an hour. He must be eager for his reward. She was certainly more than ripe.

His finger remained poised just inside her ass, waiting for her to expand. It tested her again and she smiled and bore down on it as the finger discovered it was more than welcomed.

"You can be a maestro when you want to be. My titties are so fucking hot," she said, caressing and twisting her nipples.

Jared didn't even attempt to mumble a

response. Instead he burrowed in earnest, in and out of her pussy and in and out of her ass.

Again she arched her pelvis as much as she could manage. He must know she was beyond recall. Her loins trembled like jelly and then he fondled her clit and then she lost track of what was doing what where. All she knew was she could hardly sit still. She puffed air through her lips, keeping time with that inner clock. Her hands flew to her ears trying to hold herself together.

"Oh God," she groaned, vaguely aware the chair was rocking beneath her, exaggerating every move they made. She threw her head to the side and let herself go.

She didn't know how long she'd been away before she realized her lover continued to clean her pussy with his tongue. He was no longer trying to arouse her, only tidying up. She preened and laced her fingers through his hair. She could get used to this.

"No," she cried out, sitting up abruptly pulling away from his tongue and squeezing her thighs tight.

Jared lurched away from her. The look of confusion on his face confirmed her suspicions. When had he stopped being satisfied with robust sex? Why did he want to taint sex with an irrational emotion?

Once her head had cleared she remembered feeling it in his tongue, in his fingers, in his soft moans. He'd been loving her. Was he even aware of the change?

"What's wrong?" Jared eyed her cautiously. "I thought you were enjoying that." He rose to his feet as she pushed her dress down over her thighs. "I was."

"I was to a point, but you were being nice and naughty." She stood and drew a finger along his stiff jaw line.

"I don't understand," Jared growled, grabbing her wrist.

"That's more like. Get your back up." She kissed the tip of his chin. He didn't flinch. "You were assaulting my emotions. That kind of tenderness only leads to broken hearts. I won't allow that."

"But..."

"Ssh. I like being with you, Jared. I've never been more alive sexually than I have these past several weeks, but don't go trying to turn that attraction into anything else. Understood?"

His eyes darkened, but he did nod. "Whatever the lady desires. I'll try not to assault you emotionally. You can trust me, you know."

"Good." She flashed an eyebrow. "But maybe I'm not looking for a man I can trust. Predictability is the bane of sexual relationships. Come now," she said, taking him by the hand. "It's time to pay the price for being so naughty to me."

Jared eyed Kitty with a trace of caution once he'd removed his clothes as she'd directed. She stood in the middle of the bedroom waiting for him and had made no move to strip out of her yellow dress.

His cock extended full and ready, but she probably wasn't particularly interested in his cock at the moment. He'd infuriated her on the porch. She hadn't been able to explain why, but *he* knew. She'd felt his love for her coming through his touch. So be it. He'd be more careful in the short run, but perhaps it was good she'd made that discovery.

She hadn't been completely scared off. Instead, she'd turned their emotions back into a game she could dictate.

"Kneel in the cushion chair," she ordered, "facing away from me."

He nodded, draped his arms over the back of the chair and peeked behind him. She was smiling. "Raise your ass more. That's right."

"Put your wrists together," she said, stepping around the chair. Only then did he see that she carried a leather strap, which she quickly secured around his wrists.

"That should hold you," she muttered before kissing his head. "I wouldn't want you trying to turn the tables on me midcourse. Are you comfortable enough?"

"Yeah, get on with it."

"Oh, I give the orders. Don't go anywhere—I'll be right back."

Maybe she was going to take off the dress at last. He followed her move in the mirrors that decorated her bedroom. She was clearly a woman who loved watching herself.

She rummaged through a dresser drawer before turning back to him. His eyes widened and his heart fluttered at the sight of the toys she laid out on the bed. They included a whip that appeared to be made of felt—maybe that was wishful thinking—several vibrators and dildos and a strap-on harness with a dildo in place. And there were two bottles of lube. Punishment for his transgression wasn't going to be quick.

"Getting the picture?" she asked, picking up the whip. "You've been very naughty."

She probably didn't need a reply. He clinched his butt.

"Don't be so anxious. I'm not going to hurt you. You know that. You trust me, right?"

"Sometimes," he grunted, staring at her reflection in the mirror.

"You have a very nice ass," she cooed, running her hands over his butt cheeks. "Very tight. Powerful. I love how your hamstrings stand out." Her hands slid down the back of his hips and thighs.

He winced when she hefted his balls. "Don't worry," she said, softly. "I won't do anything that will harm these boys." She reached around to skim his cock. "And how is my favorite guy? Be patient. I may get around to you."

Jared wet his lips, resigning himself to his fate. If she got around to his cock, it sure wasn't going to be anytime soon.

He saw her step to the bed and pick up a lube bottle. She smiled when she saw him watching. "It's nice having you all to myself. I can touch you anywhere and everywhere and you can't do anything about it."

"I assume that's why my wrists are bound. You're sure taking your good time about it."

"Tsk, tsk. It's a woman's prerogative to take her time. There are so many possibilities. A little preparatory work first."

Jared closed his eyes and tried not to groan when he felt the cool lube sliding down between his buttocks.

"A lava flow of lube," she cooed. "It's so thick it hardly moves. Oops. It's trying to go around your asshole. We don't want that, do we?"

"Do we?" she said, slapping his butt with an open palm.

He shook his head. He hadn't been prepared for that. He canted his eyes open and saw her beaming at him.

"I'll help," she said, softly. She made a show of wetting her finger.

He held his breath as the finger slid down his butt. He felt her covering his asshole with lube. "I better try to get a little inside," she said. "When I'm ready to fuck your ass I want you to be ready."

Her finger eased into his ass. He winced away without thinking. His reward was another stinging slap.

"You can't get away from me." She lightly kissed the flesh she'd just spanked. "Relax, Jared. Open for me. I want in."

He did his best to relax. The sooner he opened, the sooner she'd be done. "Oh my," he moaned, as her finger pushed through his outer ring. She pressed deeper and he tossed his head. He tried to reach for his cock and was quickly reminded his wrists were bound.

"You like this?" Kitty asked, sawing her finger smoothly in and out of his ass.

"Yes," he gasped.

"Good." She eased her finger out of his butt and wiped it on a cloth. "Just think how much you'll like something a lot bigger than my finger. But first things first." She winked at him in the mirror. "By the time I get around to really fucking you, you'll be begging for it."

Jared bore his head into the chair back, remembering his own words when he'd had her tied up.

He lifted his head in time to see Kitty lifting the whip above her head. Her eyes gleamed brightly. She gave him a small grin and then the whip crashed against his rear.

He jerked away from the impact. Kitty's arm rose again and he shuttered his eyes, preferring to deal with the pain in darkness rather than watch her joy. Apparently, the whip strands were made of felt, but that didn't make them painless. If only he could work on his cock. This would be so much better if he could come while she spanked him.

She had no intention of untying him. The whip fell methodically, warming both his cheeks, over and over, until they felt like she'd lit a match to them. He peeked at her through half open eyes.

She caught him looking. "That should be enough," she said, sounding winded. "For now, at least. Are they stinging a little?"

He nodded.

"This will help."

He wanted to hug her tight when she gently smoothed lotion over his butt. He knew the soothing was only a temporary way-station, but it was much appreciated.

Too soon, Kitty patted his butt and retrieved a vibrator from the bed. "We need to get you ready for the real thing," she purred, then glanced back at the strap-on still lying on the bed.

Was she trying to making him feel even more vulnerable? He shook his head. He was buck naked and she still wore her yellow dress. *That* was what made him feel vulnerable. It was as if she didn't trust herself to get that close to him.

He watched her place the vibrator in her mouth and eye him through half open eyelids. On second thought, she couldn't be any more naked. Her nipples stood out sharp and alert. And he had no doubt she was glistening wet where things really mattered.

He arched away slightly when the tip of the vibrator pressed against his anus.

"Don't," she cautioned. "Don't make things difficult." She dropped a kiss on his buttock. "I don't want to hurt you. Here we go."

"Ah, Christ," he groaned. The vibrator moved in smoothly enough. His buttocks involuntarily clenched and then softened.

Kitty withdrew the toy and winked at him. "This time I'm going to turn it on—slow speed."

The pulsating started at the outer rim of his anus. Then his asshole started to beat in time with the vibrator.

"Almost all the way," she said, over the soft hum of the toy. "Isn't that good?"

He nodded, tossing his head from side to side and squirming his butt. Everything back there was suddenly vibrating.

He didn't know she'd wrapped an arm around him until he felt her fingers gliding along his cock. He swallowed and groaned loudly. He bucked against her hand.

She laughed and withdrew her arm. "Not yet." She withdrew the vibrator and set it on a towel. "I often like to go down on a guy when I have a vibrator in his butt. Did you know your cock was vibrating? Another time. I'm sure you'd come if I

155

put you in my mouth. But we're not ready for that, are we?"

He saw no need to respond to her teasing.

She folded her arms across her abs. "Now comes a true test of how much you trust me."

He furrowed his brow.

"I'm obviously going to fuck your ass with my strap-on."

"Surprise, surprise."

She ignored him and continued, "I could fuck you where you are, but I'd prefer to see your face, since it's our first time."

He held his tongue.

"Are you going to cooperate if I move you to the bed?"

Jared let out a sigh and closed his eyes. They both knew he could overpower her easily once she released him. But that wasn't the point. He also knew this wasn't about some sort of punishment for being naughty. She wanted to fuck his ass, and had made that clear early on. She was giving him one last chance to say no.

"Okay," he said, surprised by the strain in his voice. "Show me how you want me."

- o -

Kitty smiled down at her prey. He could've gotten away easily if he'd wanted to. Jared lay on the bed with his wrists tied to the bed. His poor cock still raged about, unable to understand what was happening. She did feel sorry for his cock.

She stood at the end of the bed and saw his eyes grow huge watching her slide her hands up and down her strap-on cock, lubing it thoroughly. She'd deliberately left her shirtdress on. Only three buttons remained in place. Her breasts would likely play hide and seek once she began to move. He'd wanted her to be his vision in yellow, and that was what she'd try to be. Besides, she knew the false cock jutting out from the dress had to provide more than a little mystery. If she wound up staining the dress beyond cleaning, she'd just buy a new one. Jared's look of awe was worth much more than the price of a dress.

"You about ready for the finale?" she asked, getting quite turned on playing with her own cock. She'd already tucked a bolster under his rear end, raising it to a level that provided optimal access.

Jared smacked his lips and exhaled thinly. "Get on with it."

"Such eagerness," she said, crawling onto the bed and settling between his legs. "Raise your knees a little. That's good."

Kitty chewed on her lower lip as she brought the false cock closer to her intended target. She held her breath as she pressed its tip into Jared's ass. "Keep your eyes open," she ordered. "I want to see how this is for you. Ready for more?"

He nodded hesitantly.

She flexed her hips forward tentatively and

watched the dildo disappearing inch by inch. She paused.

"I'm doing okay."

"Good." She eased back a little and then shifted forward again, this time settling her loins against his rear. The dildo was in. Its silicone butt end pressed against her clit. She was ready to ride.

Jared's eyes were as wide as she'd ever seen them. His gaze wavered from hers, to their joining, to his rigid cock. They didn't register fear. They did reflect lust. When had he become as eager for this as she was?

She leaned forward and steadied herself on his ribcage. She flexed her butt, withdrawing the strap-on, and settled back again. "Okay?" she whispered.

He nodded. "Are you going to do this all by yourself?"

She followed his gaze to his right wrist. She chuckled. "A little help might be in order." Carefully, she leaned over and undid the band restraining his right wrist.

Immediately, Jared flexed his fingers. Then he wrapped them around his cock.

"Don't get ahead of me," she warned, "or I'll have to tie you back up."

"I'm getting used to waiting on you, woman. So are you going to fuck my ass, or what?"

Kitty laughed. She knelt back on her haunches so she could watch the false cock and Jared's hand at the same time. She undid one more dress button, fully exposing her breasts. She pulled on her nipples and smiled broadly — that simple act gave her a head start on her orgasm. She tossed her head, waiting for her nipples to trigger responses that would soon overtake her.

And then she began to ride Jared's ass. She chewed on her lower lip as she picked up speed.

"Good God," Jared howled. "What's happening?"

He bucked beneath her and stroked his cock. "Yes," she said, "I'm riding your ass. Don't wait for me."

Every time she pushed into his butt, her clit hammered against the butt of the strap-on. She tugged on her tits and bounced in and out of his ass, driving both of them insane.

"Don't stop," he cried out, "I'm almost there."

His hand had become a blur. Kitty struggled to keep her eyes open. And then she saw him erupt. Great spurts splattered his chest and hers. She thrust three more times, grinding her clit against the back of the dildo, and then she crashed.

As gently as she could, she withdrew the strap-on from Jared, unleashed its harness and tossed it aside. She felt disembodied in a rush to hold him and to be held.

She wrapped her fingers around the base of his cock. Together, they drained it. She nudged his hand away so she could take him in her mouth. Her nostrils flared with his strong scent and she refused to be denied at least a taste of his saltiness.

She wrapped an arm around his thigh and hugged him as tight as she could. His cock began to soften and retreat, but she still didn't let go.

For his part, Jared repeatedly combed her hair with his sperm covered fingers.

Dropping him from her mouth, Kitty slid up to rest her cheek on his chest and gulped for air. She couldn't recall how long she'd been holding her breath.

Her lungs filled and she breathed steadily, matching the rise and fall of his chest.

"Damn," Jared groaned. "I'm getting your hair all sticky."

She grabbed his hand. "Don't stop. It'll wash."

"I'm going to stop enough to untie my other hand, if that's okay with you."

"Oh. I forgot. Please do."

Jared gave a prolonged sigh once he was free and then he returned to combing her hair. "You have beautiful hair. So what about your dress—will it wash clean?"

She giggled against his pecs. "I doubt it. I'll buy a new one."

"Hell, if you promise to wear it while we make love—sorry, have sex—I'll buy a closet full of yellow dresses."

She chose to ignore his pointed slip of the tongue. "I could get talked into that. I am a girl who loves to shop. So did you enjoy that?" She didn't look at him.

"I did," he said after a moment. "And I also

enjoyed how much you enjoyed it." He paused and drew a finger along her cheek. "So maybe I ought to be naughty and nice more often."

Completely exhausted, Kitty wasn't about to parse words with him. Stretched out atop of him, appreciating his body warmth, she purred, "Maybe I'll have to devise some additional ways to deal with a man who refuses to obey me."

CHAPTER NINE

Standing nearly knee high in fresh straw, Jared shook each leaf of straw vigorously with the care he'd long known was important for maintaining dry bedding for horses. Ken Knowles, his friend and horse trainer, shook his head when he left Jared to muck stalls, complaining it wasn't often he had owners want to help out, but it was worth watching Jacobs doing a serious piece of work.

Groaning, Jared wasn't convinced this work was any more serious than his daily work, but he sure needed physical exercise — exercise that didn't involve a woman. On one hand, it was amazing he could still move after she'd finished with him last night. Yet by the time the sun had come up he was bursting with emotionally charged energy.

He'd left her sleeping soundly. He poked the fork into another leaf of straw and began shaking it. They hadn't talked much. He winced. They'd reeked of sex and had agreed to shower — separately. Kitty went first. She was asleep by the time he'd finished in the bathroom.

She could look so peaceful and non-threatening when sleeping. And she could be the most unpredictable woman he'd ever met when awake. Hot and cold. Mercurial. Every time he thought he was getting a fix on her, she'd duck to the left or the right.

She'd been so responsive in the rocker on the porch. If his knees had held out he'd still be eating her. He'd never seen her more relaxed and receptive.

And then all hell broke loose. She'd just about accused him of loving her too much. Out of breath, Jared leaned against the pitchfork and took a long deep lung-full of the heavy air scented with straw, manure and sweat.

She'd been methodical and persistent in reestablishing her control of their relationship. His buttocks clenched and he wet his dry lips. She'd been thorough, all right. Had she expected him to be repulsed? She'd certainly found that an acceptable risk.

He'd been with women who enjoyed dominating, but he'd never let one go as far as Kitty. Did she even consider the possibility that by upping the ante they'd only strengthened the bond between them? He'd chosen not to fight her and she'd chosen not to hurt him.

He wasn't at all certain he could've freed his wrists without her assistance. And she'd wanted him on his back when she took his ass. She didn't say it, but he knew she could have taken him easily when he was bound and kneeling in the chair.

But she'd wanted to see his reactions. If she hadn't, he would not have seen so clearly the concern etched on her face as she pressed the false cock farther into his ass. Damn. Damn. She'd been so careful, and he loved her for that. And he'd been surprised by how much he enjoyed the entire experience.

If she expected her desires would get rid of him, she was quite wrong. He wouldn't want another bout like that tonight. He grinned, looking out toward the alley way. Not tonight, but he definitely wanted a repeat performance.

Did she have any idea how she purred when she took his cock into her mouth and greedily cleaned him? An observer might be forgiven for mistaking her soft moans as sounds of love.

"You're out here awfully early."

Jared wiped straw dust from his lips and removed his leather gloves. He stepped out of the empty stall. "Morning, Lawrence. You're out rather early yourself." Jared shook the gray-haired man's hand warmly. "What brings you out here?"

"Certainly not mucking stalls."

Jared slapped his hat against his thigh and grinned at the pieces of straw flying around. "Sometimes hard work is the best medicine."

Lawrence laughed with a twinkle in his eyes. "Sounds like Kitty is getting to you. I've got a horse working out in about ten minutes. Want to come watch her with me?"

"I always like to watch morning workouts."

Jared inhaled the fresh air deeply, cleansing his nostrils and his lungs of dust. He liked the fact that Lawrence wasn't into chatter. There wasn't a better time to be at a track than early morning. The days started hectic with trainers, horses and grooms going every which way, but with a purpose. Each man and woman shared a love for the horses and many a love for the early morning sun, warming the day, providing at least a hint of hope.

Jared leaned up against the track rail as did Lawrence. He needed to get out to the track more often—especially early in the morning. He wondered what Kitty would make of the controlled chaos. He squinted at a horse and rider coming around the turn. Maybe this routine wasn't all that different from hers. She seemed to thrive on chaos.

"Is your horse out here yet?"

"Yeah," Lawrence said pointing, "she's the chestnut filly over there with the rider wearing red pants."

"Ah." Jared shielded his eyes. "Nice looking."

Lawrence chuckled. "The filly, or the rider?"

"I was speaking of the filly, but now that you mentioned it, the rider fills out those red pants quite nicely, too."

"You are hooked if you didn't notice that before I pointed her out." Lawrence spat. "I'm probably two or three decades older than you, but I tell you a guy can't get too old to notice a nice looking woman."

Jared glanced at Lawrence, who shrugged one

shoulder.

"And I'm a happily married guy."

"That's right," Jared said, looking back at the horses working. "Kitty introduced you to Rebecca."

Lawrence chuckled softly. He glanced at his stop watch and back at the track. "That's right. They'd known each other for years. Rebecca and I are compatible. I'll answer the question you want to ask, but won't. I'll always be grateful to Kitty for what she did for me."

Jared caught the corner of the man's mouth turning up in a smile.

"She showed me I still had a life left. She was too much for me to handle, but that was never the point. Rebecca and I will always hold Kitty dear in our hearts." Lawrence peered though a small pair of binoculars. "Compatibility, though, that's the key. Just like a jockey and a horse."

"Not sure I've thought of it quite like that."

"Maybe you should," Lawrence grunted, not lowering the glasses. "The high strung ones require the most sensitive hands. Got to know when to be firm and when to be soft."

Jared nodded, not quite certain whether the older man was still talking about horses or women or both.

"Well, that's it," Lawrence said, checking his watch. "Told Rebecca I wouldn't be late for breakfast. See you around."

Jared nodded and watched Lawrence Madison

stroll toward the parking lot. Compatibility must be related to punctuality.

He glanced back at the track. He and Kitty hadn't talked about breakfast. Often as not she'd catch hers on the run to an early meeting or stop for fast food fare on the way to the office.

Compatibility. Was she even looking for that? And would she know it if she found it?

He rested his hands and chin on the top rail of the fence. He inhaled through his nose. How many guys were interested in playing the kinds of games she wanted to play?

Jared grunted and straightened. So did that make them compatible? He smiled down at his hands. Could he read her well enough to know when she required soft or when she required firm?

- o -

"Why are you giving me that funny look?" Kitty had been searching through files in the file cabinet when she'd caught Maria eyeing her. The woman often acted as if she were clairvoyant, as if she knew a secret and wasn't about to tell. Now what had piqued her interest? Kitty glanced quickly around the office. Had Jared sent her more flowers?

Maria shrugged with mirth. "It's just you."

"What to you mean by that remark?" Kitty crossed her arms under her breasts and glared.

"How long have I worked for you?" Maria

looked at the ceiling as if she were counting the years.

"Too long," Kitty groaned. "You've been with me for a dozen years and we both know it. Now what are you preening about?"

Maria laughed. "That's a good one—me, preening. You're the one who's been prancing around these last several days preening with satisfaction."

"I have not."

"Oh yes, you have. I've never seen you glow like this in all the years I've worked with you. This lover must be special."

Kitty remained silent. She wanted to point out that Maria worked *for* her, not with her, but she knew better than to taunt the woman. Her office depended on Maria's organizational skills. They'd only had a couple flare ups over the years and neither had been fun.

"Well, I don't hear you denying it." Maria's eyes twinkled and her mouth bowed in a broad smile. "I'm happy for you, Kitty. It's about time you found someone special."

"Special?" Kitty tried not to come unglued. "Special? I didn't say Jared is special."

"You don't have to say it. Your body, your aura says it all."

"Right." Kitty shook her head. "There's no use trying to argue with you when you think your extrasensory talents have kicked into gear. But I'm telling you, you're wrong, and I don't want to talk about this anymore. I'll go over these files in my office."

Maria's giggles annoyed her as she walked into her office.

"You don't fluster easy, Kitty. So why are you flustered now?"

Kitty slammed the office door and stalked to her desk. She should've fired her nosy secretary years ago.

She snapped a pencil in half. What the hell was she going to do with Jared?

Nearly a week had passed since she'd set him straight for trying to overwhelm her in the rocker with his gentleness. She couldn't shake the feeling something fundamental had happened for both of them when she'd claimed his ass with her strap-on. They'd never talked about it, but something happened — something inexplicable, and she wasn't convinced it was something entirely desirable. She hadn't put on the strap-on again because she wasn't sure she could trust her own emotions.

And now he'd be going back to San Diego in a couple days. Would she miss him? She was afraid she would. Would he miss her?

He'd made it clear she had an open invitation to visit him at his ranch. She'd been more than mildly curious about where he lived and how he lived, but she didn't want to be too obvious.

Maybe she should visit her daughter and son-in-law in Seattle and then fly down to San Diego on the way back to Chicago. That would make it clear she hadn't simply made a trip to see Jared. She'd be in the area and stop by.

She smiled. Probably Jared wouldn't accept that explanation any more than Maria would, but neither would he likely challenge it.

Kitty watched Jared's cock bulging as she gently encircled it with thumb and forefinger at the base of its mushroom crown. She lay atop his strong chest. While she admired Jared's penis, his tongue and fingers toyed with her pussy without penetrating.

This was Jared's last night in Chicago. Neither of them seemed in a hurry to end it. Kitty closed her eyes and inhaled his male scent. Would it be their last night together?

"Are you going to miss me?" Jared asked from behind her.

It pleased her he hadn't asked that inevitable question when he could see her facial response. Had he done that on purpose? She flicked her tongue at the tip of his cock and it twitched back and forth. "I'll miss this guy," she said at last.

Jared's palm stung her ass cheek. "Now who's being naughty?"

"It's the truth. I will miss him." She planted a kiss on its tip. "And I may even miss his attachments a little."

"Well, that's something," Jared grunted, spreading her butt cheeks and tickling the ridge between her pussy and anus with his tongue.

She quivered and clutched his cock firmly, unsure what he would do next. Jared was proving to be a very unpredictable lover, and she liked that a lot.

He ground the heel of one hand against her vulva while lightly fingering her clit. The other hand slid along her spine and his tongue pressed against her anus.

Kitty flexed back on her knees while at the same time taking his cock into her mouth. His chuckle was nearly smothered by her flesh. She waggled her butt, wanting more.

She gripped his cock at its base and bobbed up and down only to give up quickly as his tongue rimmed her anus and dove tentatively into her widening opening. She was having difficulty multi-tasking.

His fingers strummed her throbbing clit and his tongue burrowed in and out of her ass. She shuddered, seeing first black and then red behind closed eyes. "Oh hell, tongue me," she mewed. "My ass...I'm coming." She propped herself up on both hand and widened as much as she could for him.

And then she shattered. She pulled away from his tongue and collapsed on his chest, trapping his hand between them. "No more. Please. I...you...later."

Kitty searched for the pieces of herself as she quaked and shuddered. She tried to find her bearings. She rested a cheek on his thigh. Somehow he'd retrieved his trapped hand, because he clutched her buttocks with one hand and lightly massaged her lower back with the other.

When her breathing approached normal, she swung around to face her lover. He had that smug look on his face, as if he'd gotten away with something. Then she remembered his fingers softly etching circles on her back as she recovered from her orgasm.

She chose to ignore that. This was their last night, at least for a while. But neither did she want to discuss his possessive look.

Instead she knelt and reached for his cock. "I'm sorry. I left this guy out. Sometimes I have difficulty doing two things at once."

"No problem," Jared said, reaching down to help her guide his penis up and down her wet crevice. "He knew you wouldn't forget him."

"He won't be easy to forget." Kitty rose on her knees and fell back quickly, impaling him. She smiled when she saw his rounding eyes.

"He's home now," Jared said, thrusting his hips and seating himself even deeper.

She moved to glide up his cock, but his large hands gripped her hips, holding her in place. She tilted her head to the side. "What now?"

"Are we going to remain exclusive?"

"What?" She scowled and settled back, resting on his hips. "This is a hell of moment to bring that

173

up, isn't?"

He smiled devilishly and waggled his hips. She tried to ignore his cock. "Maybe, maybe not." He wiggled again and she squirmed, not wanting him to see the effect he was having on her. "Well?"

"A month is a very long time." She tossed her head and leaned back. Two could play this game. He must have a perfect view of their joining. He didn't stop her from sliding along his hips, playing with his penis. "I can't remember when I last went an entire month without a cock."

She dropped her hand to her belly ring and then lower. Jared's gaze was fixed on her pussy and his cock. She nudged her clit with her fingers and giggled when he flinched. He freed her hips from his grasp. Had he given up? "Is my clit erect enough for you?"

Jared nodded and tugged at his mustache. "So you're not going to make that commitment."

She watched him swallow hard as she inched up his length and lowered just as slowly. "I don't want to make promises I might not be able to keep."

"But you'll try?"

She rose and fell, driving his cock deeper into her vagina. She raised her hands above her head and twisted around. She settled quickly and squinted at him. "But I refuse to feel like a failure if I can't do without."

"Hey," Kitty squealed. One moment she'd been sitting riding him, and the next she was on her back with Jared glaring down at her.

He drove into her, pushing her up the mattress.

She saw his dark expression and grinned. "You're going to fuck me real good, aren't you?"

His only response was a growl and a shake of the head. Then he reared back and slammed into her harder, with his mouth only inches from hers.

She clawed his back. "More," she mouthed.

She spread her knees as wide as she could and he pummeled her with long, smooth strokes. His palms pressed the mattress next to her head. His hard biceps loomed before her. He had her gulping for more air and space. He wasn't giving her enough of either.

She pounded his back with her fists and bucked beneath him. His eyes glazed, but he still raged on. She was no longer convinced he was even in his body. His mouth opened and closed quickly. And then his strokes became short and rapid-fire.

She sank her fingernails into his back and pummeled his ass with her heels.

"Good God," he bellowed, arching away from her without slowing his pace.

"That's right," she squealed. "Fill me. Don't let me forget you."

And then Jared began jerking. His spasms gave her pause. He'd lost control. She watched him with awe as he pumped and pumped until at last he collapsed against her breasts. Still his rump rose and fell sporadically.

Kitty hugged him close, smoothed out his hair

and rubbed his tight straining back muscles. She blinked away tears. She must've come several times in the last few minutes, but she couldn't remember for sure. She'd been so focused on Jared she'd lost track of her own responses.

Oh my. He hadn't tried to love her with his gentleness. He probably hadn't had much control over what he was doing when he went primitive on her. He snored softly and she smiled. Could a man declare his love for a woman in that way?

She didn't know about that, but it did make him more loveable. She should probably wake him up and make sure he hadn't misunderstood what they'd shared.

But she didn't have the strength or the will to do that. Not now. Later, maybe.

Kitty yawned and stretched and then snuggled as close as she could with Jared. His weight didn't bother her at all.

Two weeks later, Kitty felt the weight of the world on her shoulders. She missed him. Dammit.

She still wasn't back to her normal self. He'd called once. They'd both been incredibly tentative.

She'd wanted to whip out a vibrator and regale him with phone sex, but she hadn't. He must be waiting for her to call. She'd started to punch his numbers but something stopped her. And now she'd waited too long. Or had she?

And why did she even want to keep him in her life at all? She shook her head at her own stupidity. She'd never met a man who so completely turned her on, was willing to play all her games and who stimulated her even outside the bedroom. Jared had a mind to go along with a superb body and a ribald sense of humor.

Damn. She wasn't ready to walk away from him. There were too many possibilities yet for them to explore.

Kitty held her breath and looked at the ticket on the counter. She'd use it at least to visit her daughter and husband in Seattle. There was still time to decide whether she'd use the leg she'd reserved from Seattle to San Diego.

What would Jared say if she called him from the San Diego airport? Even she didn't have the nerve to arrive on his doorstep without some warning. He might need an hour or two to get rid of the girls he was currently entertaining. After all, he'd given her that same courtesy when he'd arrived unannounced in Chicago.

So why did she think he'd been entertaining hordes of women since his return to the ranch? She hadn't had the energy or the interest to take on another man since he'd left.

- o -

"Jared, I don't like to pry," Serena said, standing between him and his office doorway.

"No, but you will." Jared sighed, recognizing the mixture of concern, seductiveness, and curiosity. She'd dressed for seduction. Often she'd come to the office in jeans and a discreet top, appropriate for the informality of his office and for being the mother of a five year old.

This morning she'd dressed with a different sort of mission on her mind. Her nipples puckered against a thin pink top. A beige mini hardly covered much of her thighs, and she'd worn open-toed high heel sandals she knew screamed sex for him.

She closed the distance between them and laced her fingers around his neck, crushing her bosom against his chest. She kissed him full on the mouth.

Serena leaned away from him when he didn't return the kiss. "I've never seen you in such doldrums. You haven't come to visit me since you returned from Chicago."

"I see you most every day," he said, ignoring her jibe.

"That's not what I mean, and you know it," she huffed, pulling his hand up under her skirt until his palm covered her damp, bare pussy. "We've missed you."

He gasped when her hand dipped between them to fondle his rapidly growing cock. "I can't," he said, jerking away from her.

She stood before him with her balled fists on her hips. "You mean you won't." She exhaled slowly and Jared relaxed a little when he saw a smile work its way across her lips. "At least I know you're not brain dead. You still have strong vital signs." Serena stepped back and leaned against the front of her desk. "So what are you going to do about her?"

"Who?"

"Don't try to be coy with me. We've known each other too long for that. Kitty Paige—the woman who sent you the gifts. The woman who seems intent on claiming your cock for herself."

Jared shook his head. He shrugged. He sighed. Serena was right—they'd known each other for too long and been through too much for him to hide. "I called her once. She hasn't called me."

"Oh," Serena giggled. "That explains everything. It's the old male-female stare down."

Jared shrugged, seeing no need to volunteer information.

"So maybe you ought to fly back to Chicago and throw her over your shoulder and haul her ass back here."

Jared couldn't help but laugh at that image. "Kitty's not the sort of woman who'd allow a guy to cart her off like that. If there's going to be any carting off, she'll likely as not do the carting."

Serena's mouth turned up in a smile. "Sounds like my kind of woman." She folded her hands at her waist. "So what are you going to do about her?"

"I don't know. She's a hard one to figure. She may be too high maintenance for me."

"But you'll call her again."

"I might."

"She sounds pretty important to you."

He gave his petulant assistant a half smile. "She may be. Sometimes I think she's more important to me than she wants to be."

"Umm. So when are you going to bring her to the ranch for Seth and me to meet her—you do intend for us to meet her?"

He nodded. "If I can keep her from running away from me, you'll have an opportunity to meet her."

"Good," Serena said, softly moving around to sit at her desk. "I know you don't need our approval, but it would be nice to meet your lady before she becomes too territorial."

"We'll see," Jared said squaring his shoulders. "I doubt Kitty is very territorial."

Serena flashed him an eyebrow. "She's a woman, isn't she?"

He nodded.

"It takes a very strong woman—or a very strong man, for that matter—not to get hung up on territoriality. Now if you'd stop bothering me, I've got lots of work to do."

Bemused, Jared shut his office door behind him and glanced around his office. Serena was right. He should bring Kitty to the ranch, and soon.

He might be motivated to move mountains for her, but some things wouldn't change—even for her. When Serena had given birth to Savannah, the three of them—Serena, Seth and he—had agreed

virile, even given his age."

Kitty held in a cough.

"And I knew he'd seen me as a woman before." Susan squared her shoulders. "I'd paraded before him previously in my negligee and bikini, when he and Jackson had visited. He never said anything, but he didn't have to. His arousal spoke louder than words."

"So you thought you had him where you wanted him when Jackson and Brad were both out."

"Not quite." Susan smirked. "He sat on the living room couch and I flashed him."

"You exposed a boob?"

Susan shook her head. "I lifted my skirt and shimmied toward him. I wasn't wearing panties."

"No, I suppose they'd only get in the way of your plans."

Susan's eyebrows drooped into a frown. "He didn't react. He watched me bring myself off. After I cleaned my sticky fingers on his shirt, he stood. I thought he'd lay me on the floor, but he merely brushed by me, opened the door and left. He never said a word. I was so mortified."

"I'm sure Brad must've been surprised when he got back."

"Most definitely. He tried all night to make me feel better, but nothing he did could get that chuckling mustache out of my mind. The bastard. And now he's fucking my mother."

"More age appropriate, I suppose." Kitty eyed

her daughter carefully. "You'd better get used to that. And if you ever make another play for Jared, I'll scratch your eyes out myself."

"Pull your claws back in, Mom. I'm happily married. And even if I wasn't, Jared Jacobs would be the last man I'd ever try to seduce again."

"Well, that's something."

"And now that I'm getting over the shock," Susan sighed heavily, "I can be pleased for you. Where do you think this is going?"

Now it was Kitty's turn to feel uncomfortable. "Does it have to go anywhere?"

"You must be more interested than usual to visit him at his ranch. I've only been there once. It's beautiful, nestled in the foothills. Oh," Susan's eyes widened, "you haven't met Serena?"

Kitty's arms chilled. "Who's Serena?"

Susan shook her head. "She and her husband work for Jared. I think Seth manages the ranch. And they have a delightful little girl. I don't remember her name."

"Oh." Kitty let out a breath she didn't realize she'd been holding.

"Isn't it ironic," Susan said, sticking her tongue out, "you were worried I might've fucked Jared, and you fucked Jackson."

Kitty started. "You know that!"

"Of course. I knew that before you walked me down the aisle at our wedding." She smirked. "It's not every girl who's given away by a mother who fucked the best man the night before!"

Kitty groaned. "Yeah, well, that was not one of my finer choices."

"I'm sure," Susan said, rising to fill their coffee cups. "I certainly hope the father is better in bed than the son."

"I'm not going there," Kitty said, recalling vividly that Jackson had said he'd fucked Susan. "I'm not one who kisses and tells. So you're going to be okay with me flying to San Diego?"

"Does it matter?"

Kitty saw the twinkle in Susan's eyes and grinned. "Not really, but it would be nice to know you're not hating me for it."

"I'm not, Mom. I'd never hate you. And if you and Jared can make something that's lasting, that'd be wonderful. It's past time for you to find someone who tolerates you enough to actually set up house with you."

"That's not what I'm after," Kitty sputtered, spilling her own coffee.

Susan handed her several napkins. "Sometimes we don't know what we're after until it finds us."

Kitty stopped soaking up the spilled coffee to glare at Susan. "And when did you become a voice of wisdom?"

Susan smirked. "I may be younger, but I'm not without experience. Besides, I've had you to watch all my life. You inspire wisdom."

"Right. I didn't know I raised such a bullshit artist."

"It's okay," Susan said, gripping her hand.

"Thanks for everything, Mom. And I do want you to have fun. When you see Jared, give him our best wishes. With you on his doorstep, he'll need them."

Kitty dug in her purse for her cell phone. Instead she pulled out a brush and ran it through her curls, then freshened her lipstick. She sat in the San Diego airport kicking herself for not having called before she left Seattle. Jared could be halfway around the world, for all she knew.

Or he could be buried under several female bodies.

Letting out a deep sigh, she hit the number on the cell phone. She'd come this far—she wasn't about to turn back now.

"Well, hello." Jared's deep voice calmed her aching nerves. He probably had caller I.D.

"Hi," she said, as lightly as she could.

"I was wondering if you'd ever call."

"Well, I am." She hesitated. "I'm at the airport."

"O'Hare?"

She could hear his frown through the cell. She shook her head. "Nope. San Diego International."

"San Diego," he gasped. "You're here. Son of a bitch."

"Is that a good son of a bitch, or an *I wish you'd stayed in Chicago* son of a bitch?"

"I'm elated. Thrilled. Where are you? I'll come pick you up."

"Terminal One, but I can get a hotel if this isn't

convenient for you."

"Nonsense. Damn, this is the best news since...since I left Chicago. I'll be there within the hour. How will I find you? Are you wearing yellow?"

"Of course. Just for you. I'm wearing a replica of that yellow shirtwaist dress we so thoroughly destroyed."

His chuckle tingled in her ear. "That's fantastic. Are you wearing anything under it?"

"Jared, I've been flying. Of course I'm wearing panties."

"Ditch them." His voice sank low. "If not now, at least when you get to the ranch. I don't want you wearing anything that might impede us while you're at the ranch."

She chuckled. "House rules?"

"Ranch rules."

"I'll do my best," she said sweetly, "to follow your rules while I'm out here. After all, I am a guest. I wouldn't want to get into trouble while away from home."

"You're already in trouble for not giving me more notice."

"Did I catch you with your harem?"

"Not hardly. But I would've spruced up the place if I'd known you were coming."

"So I'm already in trouble," she teased, twirling strands of hair around her finger. "My rear is quivering with anticipation."

"Don't go getting ahead of me," he growled.

"I'll be there as soon as I can. Bye."

"Bye," she whispered into the phone. She rose to her feet and headed toward the nearest restroom. She might as well ditch the panties. She grinned. Maybe she should've called him before she'd packed for the trip.

Kitty glanced quickly at Jared when he brought the car to an abrupt stop on the u-shaped gravel driveway at the end of which stood a classic low slung adobe ranch house with a tiled roof. To her right were three smaller buildings and to the left was a long building she assumed was a stable.

"What is it?" she asked, "Isn't that your house?"

"It is," he growled. "I forgot the damn carpet cleaners were coming this afternoon."

She watched him stare across her toward one of the out buildings. She followed his line of sight to catch a glimpse of someone backing away from a curtain.

"Son of a bitch." He gave her a hungry look. He squeezed her bare thigh and gave her a curious smile. "You once said you wouldn't mind finding a horse stall. I hope you still don't, because I'm sure as hell not going to wait another four hours."

His mouth crushed against hers. She wrapped her arms around his neck and responded eagerly. His hand slid along her thigh until it found her damp exposed pussy. His finger met with no resistance as it drove home.

"Oh," she moaned into his ear rocking her pelvis. "I think…oh…I'd prefer the horse stall to this cramped seat."

"Sorry," he said, pulling away from her.

She clutched his hand and eased him out slowly. "Too bad he can't stay."

"We won't be long."

They both clambered out of the car and Jared grabbed her hand and dashed toward the stable. Glancing back at the car, Kitty gave up on the idea of grabbing a bag. She turned back to focus on where Jared was half leading, half dragging her, but not before she once again saw movement behind a curtain in the building nearest the house. Someone was more than a little curious about what they were up to. She didn't care. She was so hot for Jared they could fuck in front of a full coliseum, as long as they fucked soon.

- o -

Jared pulled off his boots and shucked his jeans as he watched Kitty slowly lift the yellow dress over her head. Could she be even more beautiful than he remembered?

She handed him the folded dress. "Put this somewhere safe," she said, "I didn't bring a replacement."

He put the dress aside and stepped out of his boxers. Her rounding eyes pleased him immensely. He drew her into his arms; his cock

191

nestled against her loins and she teased his nipples by drawing hers across them. "I hope this isn't too rustic for you," he whispered. "We don't have an empty stall, but this tack room should work."

"I love the smell of leather and saddle soap," she said, sliding her lips along his collar bone. "So now that we're here, what do you have in mind? We could just stand in place, I suppose."

Jared shook his head.

"We could spread out several horse blankets — though I suppose they're quite smelly."

"For good reason," he said, shifting his gaze from her to the corner.

Her gaze followed his. Her eyebrows arched high. "We can't..."

He caught the eager curiosity in her tone as she considered the western saddle sitting on a small dummy horse. "Uhm. The saddle has possibilities. Your feet will touch the floor."

"Oh my," she murmured. "I'm getting the picture, if not the feel of it. Will it hold us?"

"Of course it will." Jared quickly pulled the dummy out into the center of the tack area, not giving Kitty much chance to think.

"I'll get on first," he said, throwing a leg over the saddle and settling back into its cantle. He stroked his penis in case Kitty had lost track of what they were doing.

He watched her weigh the merits of the saddle before she lifted a leg over the front of the saddle to face him. "I thought western saddles had saddle horns," she said, sliding along the saddle and grabbing his cock with both hands.

"Some do. Some don't. This one doesn't. It'll work with or without. Now that we're here," he said, lifting a boob in each of his palms, "do you have any more ideas?"

Kitty leaned over to kiss the tip of his nose and then his mustache and then his mouth, all the while squirming her crotch against his penis. If she didn't do more for his cock damn soon, he'd have to take control.

"Oh, this is so good," Kitty cooed, rising off the saddle and rubbing his penis along her pussy. She arched higher on her toes and inserted the crown of his cock.

Jared tried to breathe evenly.

She winked at him. "Is this what you've been waiting for?"

He nodded. "Haven't you?"

She ran her tongue along her lower lip and took more of him in. She paused, waiting. "When we dashed in here, I felt like we were acting like a couple teenagers."

"And now?"

"I never had it this good when I was a teen."

He watched her catch her breath and lower herself a little farther down his shaft. She wobbled. He clasped her hips to steady her. She raised her arms above her head and beamed down at him. And then she raised her torso only to quickly slam down against his hips, taking his full length in deep.

"Oh," she groaned, rocking in the saddle slightly. "I've missed this guy so much. And you're right, this is an incredible angle. You ready for your cowgirl to go for a ride?"

He nodded. "Any time you're ready." He did like the fact she'd referred to herself as his cowgirl. Was that a slip? He watched her close her eyes and slowly weave her body side to side and back and forth, testing their joining.

Jared peered up at the tiny security camera. He was sure Serena was enjoying this little tableaux nearly as much as he and Kitty were. She probably had two or three fingers buried in her pussy, ready to time her climax with theirs.

He turned his attention back to Kitty and twisted her nipples and she immediately moaned her appreciation. Would she enjoy watching as much as Serena did?

"Here we go," Kitty announced. She opened her eyes and smiled down at him. She rose on the balls of her feet and settled back down, encasing his cock. "I'm not going to stop until I've milked you dry. So hang on."

He didn't doubt her for a second. He held out his hands and she placed one of hers in each of his, bracing herself. She increased her tempo. Her breasts bobbed and her mouth twisted into a pinched smile. She had nearly all the leverage. There wasn't much for him to do but watch and feel. He flexed his hips as much as he could and she drove faster, harder and deeper.

Her whimpers told him what he wanted to know. This wasn't just about him. She clamped her vaginal muscles around him. Jared threw back his head and howled.

"Gotcha." She laughed, not slowing a bit.

"Oh fuck," he groaned. His toes curled against the cement floor. His hamstrings burned, then the head of his cock blew.

"I feel him spurting," she squealed, reclaiming a hand to claw at her clit.

His upper torso jerked forward and backward, trying to help. He fought for air. "I can't stop coming."

"I want it all," she commanded.

He gave up watching, helping, doing anything. She'd propelled him into space. Her cries of ecstasy penetrated his haze. Her efforts slowed. She crashed to his chest and he wove his fingers through her hair. Still they rocked back and forth as if he had any more for her to claim.

He shuddered as her hot breath soothed his nipples. She licked the perspiration from his neck. At last he cranked an eye open to see her grinning broadly.

"Hi," she said. She nipped at his mustache. "I've never aspired to be a cowgirl, but I could get used to this."

He pecked at the corner of her mouth and slid a hand down her backside, pleased to feel her trembling. He patted her butt. "You sit a saddle very nicely. We might want to try one with a saddle horn later."

"Much later," she purred in his ear. "So now that we have this urgent need taken care of, are you going to show me your ranch? After we recover, of course."

"That may take a while. Are you comfortable enough?"

"Absolutely."

"Welcome to the ranch," Jared drawled, kissing her hair. "I hope you'll like it."

"It certainly started off with a bang," she chuckled. "I don't know how it can get better than this."

Kitty's breathing slowed. He let her nap. She'd certainly earned it, but he hoped it would get better for her than even this. He peered at a security camera wondering briefly what Serena made of his latest houseguest.

- o -

"It's so huge," Kitty breathed, shading her eyes from the setting sun. "You own all of this?"

"Yes." Jared leaned against the pickup he'd used to chauffer Kitty around his ranch. "Just about, anyway. Still, the ranch considerably smaller than it used to be."

"So much space. My eyes are straining trying to find the horizon."

196

"Come on," he said, grabbing her by the hand. "Let's get back to the house. The carpet guys should be gone by now."

She climbed into the truck, letting him help her. How long had it been since a man even held a door for her? Jared Jacobs surprised her at moments like this. He could be a throwback to a more chivalrous era, and yet he was as bold and adventurous as any lover she'd ever known. He'd have his way with her, yet he'd let her take charge, too. They were a good match in that way. Neither one of them needed to be in control all the time.

He climbed in the driver's seat and she held on tight as the truck bounced down the dirt ruts leading back toward the buildings. This was no time for small talk. She'd be lucky if her teeth didn't crack.

"That was a little rough," Jared said, pulling onto a smooth lane. "This will be better."

Kitty surveyed the house and outer building again as they approached. She leaned forward when she caught glimpse of a redheaded woman chasing an equally redheaded child. The woman was laughing as hard as the child.

When they scampered back toward a porch, Kitty realized one of the outbuildings wasn't an outbuilding at all — it was the front of another long rambling house. She was about to ask Jared if that was the woman and girl Susan had told her about when Jared waved at the woman and started to get out.

"Climb on down," he said, "here's some folks I want you to meet."

As soon as Jared cleared the truck the little girl ran and jumped, evidently trusting Jared would indeed catch her. Which he did, and then he twirled the giggling girl around in circles before setting her carefully down on her feet.

"Savannah," he said to the girl, "this is a friend I want you to meet. Her name is Kitty."

Shyly the little girl stuck out her hand and Kitty dropped to her knees to take it. "Good to meet you, Savannah. How old are you?"

"I'm five," she announced, puffing out her small chest. "I have a kitty. Are you Uncle Jared's kitty?"

Kitty glanced up at Jared and the woman who must be the girl's mother. Jared looked smug. The woman's eyes sparkled like diamonds. No help was coming from either one.

"I doubt your uncle Jared needs another kitty," she finally answered.

"He doesn't have a kitty like you."

"That's enough, Savannah," her mother scolded. "Hi, I'm Serena Sampson, and this is my daughter. She can be a pest at times."

"No problem. I'm Kitty Paige. Pleased to meet you."

"Kitty is Susan's mother," Jared interjected. "You met Susan, I believe, when she and Brad visited Jackson out here."

"Of course I did. Your daughter's beauty nearly

matches your own."

Kitty felt a small blush creep up her cheeks. The redhead, although dressed in jeans and a pullover top, was a stunner herself, but Kitty saw no need to extend this mutual admiration moment. She glanced quickly at Jared, who appeared quite amused by something.

"I've yet to show Kitty the house. I'm sure the two of you will have a chance to chat before she leaves."

"How long will you be visiting us?" Serena asked, giving her a half smile.

The question caught her off guard and seemed too familiar, but maybe there was something about westerners being more friendly and open with strangers than their counterparts in the east. "I'm not sure," she replied. "I haven't discussed that with Jared yet. A few days, I imagine."

"Good." Serena smiled easily. "We'll want to do a cookout while you're here, and maybe you'll want to go into to town and do some shopping. I hope I'm not being too forward, but we don't see many other women out here. This is pretty much a man's place."

"So I've noticed." So that explained Serena. Lonely for female companionship. "I'm sure I'll want to go shopping."

"Get back in," Jared said. "We'll park up at the house."

"Bye," Kitty said, waving at the girl.

Jared stepped over and whispered something in

Serena's ear. The woman laughed and nodded. Kitty thought she heard her say, "crystal clear."

When Jared climbed in behind the wheel, he explained, "Serena has worked in my office," he pointed toward the building nearest the house, "for years. Her husband manages the ranch. I couldn't hold onto this place without them."

CHAPTER ELEVEN

"This place is heavenly," Kitty sighed, rolling over onto her back on the chaise lounge. The tiny scraps of fabric covering her breasts and crotch hardly seemed necessary. For the past two days she hadn't seen another soul come near the house. It was as if she and Jared were at their own private resort. He'd done the cooking, with her assistance. And they'd made marvelous love—on the patio, in his mammoth bedroom, and on the freshly cleaned carpets. They'd been gentle and then rough or rough and then gentle. She felt sated—well, almost.

"I'm glad you like my home. But then you bring more than a touch of heaven to the place yourself."

She stared softly at him through her dark sunglasses. "You can be a romantic."

"Does that bother you?"

She stretched a leg. "Not as much as it used to. I'm learning that's simply part of who you are."

"That's progress, I guess."

She tried not to read too much into that comment as Jared sat up and gave her another of those devastating grins of his. "Come on," he said, "the pool has some shade. Let's swim. Last one in…"

She didn't hesitate and raced him to the pool. She shrieked with laughter as they hit the water at the same instant. The pool was a huge plus. She seldom got to a pool in Chicago. The Lake was often too cold and was only available for swimming a few months a year.

They swam a half a dozen laps and then floated side by side. This was beyond heaven. She closed her eyes and moved in and out of awareness.

"Hey, bro." Jared's voice jolted her alert. "Come on in, the water's fine."

Kitty wet her lips and studied the stocky Adonis who stood at the water's edge. His bare chest rippled with muscles and his bare feet only contributed to his sexiness. The jeans he wore had seen better days.

She watched the man shake his head without taking his gaze from hers.

"I'm not wearing a swim suit."

"So hop in with your underwear," Jared said lightly.

Again the man shook his head. "Ain't wearing any."

"Hell, come on in anyway. The lady won't mind." Jared eyed her quickly. "Will you?"

She wet her lips and shook her head in agreement.

The Adonis didn't need a second invitation. She watched him turn around and slide his jeans down over a tight butt. He must own a swim suit. He was tan except for a very small portion of white skin that probably did nothing to hide his assets.

He turned around and slid quickly into the water, but not before she saw his very turgid cock. She stared at the stranger as he did three laps before rolling over to paddle in their direction.

"Water's fine," he said, looking at Jared. "How come I'm the only one without a suit?"

Jared laughed and wiggled his suit down his thighs before Kitty had a chance to think straight. His cock sprang immediately erect. Jesus. Jared knew she liked two cocks. Was this a set up?

"You're game, right?" Jared said, beginning to untie the knot on the right side of her bikini bottom.

She nodded and wasn't at all surprised to feel another set of hands working on the knot on the other side. She reached behind her and quickly dispensed with the top.

Jared stood in front of her and slid his cock along the crevice of her pussy. The man behind her reached around and fondled her breast. His cock nestled in the crack of her ass.

"Our Kitty loves two cocks," Jared said, just above a whisper. "Don't you?"

"Yes." She rocked back and forth between the two cocks. The buoyancy of the water made it difficult to keep them in place.

Jared led her across the pool and climbed onto the side. He grabbed his cock and stroked it for her. She nodded and moved between his legs. She leaned over and guided him to her mouth, giving the man behind her a perfect view of either target he wanted.

When she heard the other man groan and felt the head of his penis press at her vulva, she smiled around Jared's cock. She held steady and the man pushed forward, sinking his shaft into her channel. Jared's cock muffled her groan.

She waggled her rump, becoming comfortable with this new cock. Then when she was ready, she bobbed her mouth up and down Jared's shaft. He laced his fingers in her hair. The man behind her grabbed her by the thighs and hoisted her as if he was holding a wheel barrel. She was suspended on two cocks, with water supporting much of her weight. And then the water roiled as the man behind her began fucking in earnest. Each time he slammed into her she sank farther down Jared's cock. If there was ever going to be finesse among the three of them, it had already happened.

The man behind eased a little to time his thrusts with her movements along Jared's cock. When she slowed, so did he. When she quickened, he quickened too. Kitty mewled, breathing haphazardly through her nose.

She caught movement out of the corner of her eye. She started to lift off of Jared but he held her head firmly in place. The man behind her no longer followed her pace. His fingers dug into her thighs. She could feel his cock expanding.

Kitty lost herself with both cocks but couldn't

completely ignore the redheaded Serena, sitting on the edge of a lounge chair, bringing herself off. Serena's fingers became a blur. The man behind her bellowed and pulled out to splatter warm come over her backside. Her feet again touched the bottom of the pool.

"Now me," Jared grunted, helping propel her head up and down his cock. "Oh hell," he hollered.

Fingers from behind clawed at her clit as Jared filled her throat. She dropped Jared and buried her head in his lap as she quivered and quaked. "Oh my God," she whimpered, trying not to lose awareness.

She opened and shut her eyes, breathed through her straining nostrils, and stood. She glanced at the patio chairs. Serena was nowhere to be seen.

The man who had been behind her was pulling himself up out of the pool. Without a word or a glance, he slipped into his worn jeans and left.

"What the hell?" she said, looking at Jared.

He held out a hand and helped her out of the pool. "You enjoyed?" he asked.

"Yes, but…"

"Ssh," he said, slanting a finger across her lips. "Let it be. Just accept. You know what curiosity did to the cat."

Jared helped her to a blanket. Her heart still beat rapidly and she continued to gulp in air.

He lay down beside her and snuggled tight.

"You're something real special," he murmured, drying her with another bath towel.

She couldn't hold off sleep. There was so much to sort out, but she didn't have the energy to think and certainly not to mentally fence with Jared.

She let herself go, trusting her world wouldn't be any more confused when she woke from her nap. She clenched her butt, which still throbbed. Damn, she was a glutton for two cocks.

- o -

Jared held Kitty close. She'd rolled away from him as soon as they'd gone to bed. He realized neither one of them likely wanted another bout of lovemaking, but Kitty had been rather quiet since the late afternoon encounter in the pool. She'd surprised him with her lack of questions.

When they were finished in the pool she'd looked as sated as he'd ever seen her. That, in itself, was noteworthy.

He dropped a kiss on her shoulder. "I know you're still awake."

She shrugged.

He hoisted a leg over hers and ground his semi-hard cock against her rump.

"I'm done for the day," she murmured, not turning to face him.

"I know. So am I. Just letting you know he'll be around when you want him next."

"Did you know she was on the patio watching,

finger fucking herself?"

Jared stiffened. So that was it. He didn't have eyes in the back of his head, and he hadn't heard Serena come onto the patio. He probably wouldn't have heard a Mack truck, with all the splashing in the water and the throbbing in his head. "I didn't know she was there, but Serena does like to watch."

"I'm not into women."

"You told me before. Neither is Serena."

After a prolonged silence, Kitty murmured, "Oh."

Jared couldn't tell if she was surprised or disappointed.

"So I guess exclusive only applies for you when you're away from the ranch."

He was surprised by the pain lacing Kitty's tone. He slid his tongue along her collarbone before responding. She shivered and he smiled. "You're jumping to conclusions. I haven't been with Serena since we agreed to remain exclusive for the time being. I must admit I was beginning to wonder if that agreement held, after you didn't call."

"And you haven't fucked Serena since before…?"

"Ask her, if you want. She's not thrilled about that."

Kitty emitted a soft giggle. "I suppose not."

"Any more questions?"

"Who's Savannah's father?"

Jared tried to keep tension out of his voice and his body. "Does that matter?"

"Probably not. Just curious."

"Thought we talked about you and your penchant for curiosity. To answer your question, we decided we didn't want to know. Now," he said evenly, "I'm done with Twenty Questions, if you don't mind."

"Sorry," Kitty said, finally rolling over to face him. She placed a hand on each of his cheeks and kissed him softly.

Jared tried not to melt from this sudden change—Kitty had never kissed with such tenderness.

She nibbled at the corners of his mouth. "Sorry if I overstepped by prying too much. I'm not trying to judge. And from what I've seen, someone is doing a very good job of parenting with Savannah."

"Thanks," he chuckled. "Maybe there's an advantage in having three parents."

Kitty kissed his neck. "There were many times with Susan that I wished she had three parents concerned about her welfare."

Kitty propped her herself on an elbow and grinned broadly. "I'm sure I deserve a sound spanking for prying so much."

"You've earned it," he grunted.

"But not now," she said, "I'm too bushed even for that. In the morning, if you can wait that long."

"I can wait," he growled. "I might not get to

sleep thinking about it, but I can wait."

"And do you have a woodshed to take me behind?"

He laughed at her wide-eyed look of feigned innocence. "The bedroom will do fine. So were you turned on watching Serena bring herself off?"

"A little," Kitty admitted. "But so much was going on I didn't really pay much attention to her." She kissed the tip of his nose. "It was exciting, though, knowing we were being watched. Night-night."

He hugged her close when she again turned and pressed her backside against him. He patted her bottom lightly. "Sweet dreams. Until the morning."

The next morning, looking much refreshed, Kitty stepped out of the bathroom and stretched in front of him. Standing on her toes, she pulled on her nipples. "I'm ready," she announced. "Where do you want me?"

"Are you sure?" Jared closed the distance between them and gathered her in his arms. He trailed his fingers down her back until he cradled her buttocks.

Kitty snaked a hand between them to gently squeeze first his balls and then his cock. She leaned back to meet his gaze. "This guy," she said, peeking down at his penis, "seems revived."

She pushed out of his arms and bent over to plant a kiss on his soft crown. She straightened.

"My pussy and mouth are still sore from yesterday's play. Perhaps once you have my backside warmed up enough, you'll want to let this guy claim my ass again. It's been a while. I'm already lubed for him."

"You do plan ahead. Why don't you kneel on the floor and stretch over the bed?"

"That sounds lovely," Kitty said, dropping to her knees and crushing her breasts against the bed. She craned her neck and grinned. "Like this?" She waggled her ass.

"Excellent." Jared stood beside her and brushed his fingertips along her back from her shoulder to the crest of her rump. He repeated that simple gesture several times, watching Kitty's flesh quiver with anticipation.

"Are you going to tickle me to death, or paddle me?"

"Are you trying to tell me what to do?" He made a show of glowering at her.

"Oh, now I am so scared," she said, playing her own game. "Is my cowboy going spank my butt and fuck my ass?"

"Damn." He smacked her ass and she yelped. "You sure have a mouth."

She turned to look at him and smiled. "I haven't heard you complaining about my mouth. Are you complaining now?"

Again he slapped her butt before answering. "I'm not complaining—though you might want to shut up now so I can concentrate on what I'm doing."

His palm connected with her right butt cheek, stinging his hand and no doubt her ass. His hand print was quite apparent on her soft flesh. "Damn," he grunted.

"I'm fine," Kitty purred. "Super. You're not going to quit on me, are you?"

"Son of a bitch," Jared muttered, rapidly slapping one cheek and then the other. He maintained a steady cadence. At least that seemed to quiet Kitty. She squirmed her butt some and tossed her head back and forth. Her ass had turned red under his steady barrage. Perspiration clouded his vision. Would she ever admit she'd had enough?

"So good," Kitty yelled. "In my ass," she whimpered. "Jared, I need you in my ass."

Jared nodded and smiled. She probably wasn't going to give him any greater praise for paddling her ass to her liking. He grabbed the lube bottle and applied some to his eager cock before moving to stand behind her.

She spread her legs, clearly expecting him to kneel, but he didn't. Instead, he remained standing and moved up to straddle her butt. She peeked around when he tapped his cock against her dark portal.

"You wanted to be ridden," he explained. "Here I am. Your cowboy at your service." He didn't wait for her to respond but pushed his cock head into her entrance.

"Oh, yes," she sang out. "You are going to be so deep."

He didn't have long to wait before she opened for him and he sank farther into her heated channel. She arched her head back and moaned. "You okay?" he asked.

She nodded. "He's never been this deep. Give him a try."

Jared flexed back on his heels watching his penis reappear and then he flexed inward, watching it disappear again. His heart pounded. He wouldn't last long this time, but he didn't think that mattered. He quickened his tempo.

"Oh damn, damn," Kitty groaned. And then she began rocking on her knees. "Come on cowboy, ride me."

Jared settled into a steady pace, wanting to prolong the inevitable as long as possible, but he couldn't ignore Kitty's shouts: "Ride me. Ride me. Ride me!"

Jared leaned over to dig his fingers in her shoulders. And then he erupted, spilling into her.

"Yes, ride me. Fill me. Ride me."

Kitty's words were softening. Was it her, or his ears? He continued to spasm inside her as he stretched out across her back. Her body shook beneath him.

Minutes later, he stood long enough to gently withdraw from her and then they both collapsed crosswise on the bed.

She stroked his chin and his mustache.

"Magnificent," she murmured. She giggled.

"Now what?"

"I wish I'd thought of having you wear your western hat."

He kissed the tip of her nose. "Guess that would've been better than spurs."

"Ouch." She winced, then sobered. "You know I'm going to have to go back to Chicago one of these days."

"Thought you might. But not today."

"No, not today."

"I believe Serena is planning a cookout for tonight. She does think you're good for me."

"A lot she knows." She smirked. "Of course the real question is, are *you* good for me?

"I seemed to be a few minutes ago."

"Umm. Very good."

"Are you beginning to wonder if we might have something that could last?"

Her brow furrowed. "Don't push me, Jared. Let's be happy with the moment."

"Okay. But you have to know I'm beginning not to like the idea of having moments without you in my life."

"You've just never had a woman who likes playing as much as I do."

He leaned back and gave her a meaningful stare.

"Oh, I forgot. I imagine the redhead is spitfire in bed."

Jared chuckled softly. "The two of you are well

matched, actually. Too bad neither of you is into women."

"Dream on." She arched an eyebrow. "But I suppose I'll have to have a woman to woman talk with Serena to clear the air. I don't want anyone to have unrealistic expectations about me..." she hesitated, "or about us."

- o -

When Kitty entered Jared's outer office, Serena showed no surprise at seeing her visitor. Kitty knew Serena's routines well enough to know she wouldn't leave for another hour or so to drive into town to pickup Savannah. And Jared was out somewhere on the ranch "taking care of things." Probably he didn't want to be around if she and Serena got into a catfight. That didn't seem likely, but then she probably understood women better than Jared did.

"I've been expecting you," Serena said politely. "Would you like some coffee or tea? The coffee is decaf, this late in the day."

"Then I'll have some coffee," Kitty replied, wanting to keep things friendly. She familiarized herself with the large outer office while Serena came around her desk to pour coffee. The space exuded comfort, with a couch and easy chair as well as the more standard file cabinets and desk. Kitty noticed the toy box in the corner and smiled. "You have a cute little girl," she remarked, studying pictures of Savannah. She chuckled at crayon drawing of what appeared to be a fire eating dragon. "And she has quite the imagination."

"That she does," Serena said, handing her a cup. "If you want cream or sugar, I'll let you do the honors."

Kitty sipped the coffee and shook her head. "This is how I like it."

"Why don't you have a seat on the couch?" Serena claimed the easy chair. "I assume this is not merely a get acquainted visit."

"We're not exactly strangers." Kitty smoothed out the long skirt she wore. She'd been so accustomed with going commando for Jared she'd forgotten she wore no panties until she sat down. The long skirt would conceal her pussy from Serena, but that didn't keep her from tingling down there. "Do you watch all the women Jared brings to the ranch—when he makes love to them?"

Serena's lips parted slightly. "He doesn't bring that many here, but when he does, I do like to watch."

"I see."

"But they don't usually know I'm watching."

Kitty scowled.

"I can be quite discreet. And we do have a bank of security camera screens off this room." She pointed toward a door Kitty hadn't particularly noticed.

"Security cameras?" Kitty chilled—had she been spied on? "Where?"

"None inside the house," Serena cautioned. "Jared wouldn't allow that. But these race horses are expensive, and there is concern for corporate espionage. So there are cameras trained on the perimeter of the house and the other out buildings, the stable," Serena's face lit up, "and the tack room."

"No...you watched us in the tack room?"

"You sit a saddle very nicely."

What? How could Serena be so matter-of-fact? "You could've stayed in here and watched the scene at the pool."

"That's right."

Kitty leaned forward and wet her lips. "But you wanted me to know you were watching?"

"You are quick. That's right."

"Why? Why would you bother? Jared tells me you're not into women."

"I'm not—in that way. I do enjoy watching a woman use her body to love a man, or watching a skilled man bring a woman to the peak of pleasure."

"But your voyeur joys could've been satisfied without showing yourself. You haven't answered my question. Why?"

"I don't particularly care when Jared brings his women here. That's his prerogative. They go as quickly as they show up." Serena tilted her head to the side. "You're different than the others. I knew that even before I saw you. Jared's being involved with another woman has never kept him out of my bed — until now."

"He wasn't lying."

"Lying isn't Jared's strong suit. And you're right, I wanted you to come and see me." Serena sipped her coffee before continuing. "I'm quite willing to share my husband's cock with you."

"Your husband?" Kitty squeaked. She covered her open mouth.

"Who did you think was fucking you so thoroughly from behind in the pool? Seth enjoyed it as much as you clearly did. And as I said, I don't mind sharing."

"But..."

"But it's not fair for you to have two cocks and Jared just one pussy." Serena pouted like a wounded teen.

Kitty giggled. "I think I'm beginning to understand. It's also not fair for me to have two cocks and you one."

"Exactly. Have you ever watched a man and woman make love?"

"Not in person. Videos, of course."

"In person is much better. You can hear the soft purrs and flesh slapping flesh, and you can inhale the scent of sex."

"I guess your security cameras aren't wired for sound."

Serena shook her head. "Not yet." She paused. "Savannah has a sleepover this weekend. She's going directly to her friend's house after school. I'll be cooking out for us tonight."

"Too bad Savannah will miss the cookout."

"I don't want to drive you away. I only want to share. For that to happen, we have to be comfortable with each other."

Kitty squeezed the bridge of her nose as Serena rolled her skirt up to her waist, revealing a soft pussy line with close cropped reddish curls.

"I've thought of going completely bare like you, but I don't know. What do you think?"

"You sure you're not trying to seduce me?"

Serena shook her head. "No, but if we're going to share cocks then we must be comfortable with each other's nudity. And as I'm sure you know, neither of my men wants his women wearing panties any more often than absolutely necessary." Serena frowned. "Didn't you compare notes with other girls like this when you were in school?"

"That was a long time ago. You're not going to want me to watch you masturbate, are you?"

"Heavens no," Serena protested. "Anyway, I believe you've already witnessed that. Not without at least one of the guys with us. That's one of my rules."

"This little Garden of Eden certainly has a lot of rules," Kitty huffed, getting to her feet. "As for your pussy, I think it's quite attractive the way it is. Of course, if you decide to trim more, it can always grow back."

"Yours isn't plucked, then."

"No, I don't like burning bridges that much." Kitty smoothed out her skirt, hoping the younger woman wasn't going to come over and want a peek. "So I guess I'll see you this evening. Thanks for the coffee."

Serena laughed and stood, her skirt falling back down to hide her crotch from view. "It's not like I haven't seen yours. But I can wait to get a closer look."

Kitty nodded and left without further comment. She filled her lungs with mountain air as soon as she stepped out of the office. And she thought *she* was comfortable living in her own skin. Had she ever met anyone as comfortable with her own skin as Serena?

Plus, the woman had a very keen sense for fairness. Kitty laughed, flashing on the image of the blindfolded statue of justice holding the balancing scales in her hand. She'd never before wondered if that woman was a redhead, or went commando.

CHAPTER TWELVE

Filling another dip bowl for their picnic, Kitty listened to Jared coming down the stairs. She hadn't talked with him since he'd come back. He'd shouted *hi* and dashed up to shower before Seth and Serena came over with the main dish.

Kitty rechecked the sauces and her specialty, a salad. She'd already packed a cooler she'd found with soft drinks and beer. She looked toward the kitchen archway. She was ready. She breathed deeply. At least, she hoped she was.

Jared came to a sudden stop when he entered the kitchen. "You are hot!" He moved across the kitchen to grasp her hand and turn her about.

"You like?" she murmured.

"Why are we bothering with food? Sexy," he drawled, moving back to get a better look. "I doubt many women wear high heels to a picnic."

"I love high heels. And they're not too dressy, because they're sandals."

"They're sexy. That's all that matters." He reached out to touch a gold hoop earring. "Nice touch. I haven't seen these before."

"Susan helped me pick them out in Seattle. I'm glad you like them."

"They go well with the diamond belly ring." He kissed her forehead. "Have I ever told you how much I love your bare midriff?"

She laughed and tugged on his shirt. "I believe you have, but then a girl can never get too many compliments."

He rubbed a thumb over her nipples. "Are these ladies peaking for me, or are they dreaming about what might happen later?"

"I'm not telling," she said, trying not to smile.

"And are you commando?" Jared didn't wait for her response. He slid a hand up her bare thigh and under the miniskirt she'd selected with considerable care.

She leaned her head against his chest as he cupped her mound.

"Damn, are you always so wet?"

"Lately," she murmured, tucking a hand between them to help him insert a finger. "Ah," she moaned, clamping down on his finger. "Going commando certainly has its plusses." She wiggled against his finger as he probed deeper. "So," she said, eyeing him, "do you miss her pussy?"

"What the hell?" Jared startled. His features darkened and he tried to withdraw his finger, but Kitty held it firmly in place.

"Don't move. It's okay. Do you miss Serena's pussy? I just want to know."

Jared blew air through compressed lips. "Why the hell do women ask so many questions?"

"Well?"

"Of course I do. I won't lie to you about that."

"Thank you," Kitty said, "that's all I wanted to

know. Oops," she backed away from a befuddled Jared, "sounds like company has arrived."

- o -

Jared tried to keep track of the byplay between the two women as they set up the food table on the patio. Their behavior reminded him of two pups circling each other trying to determine an edge or weakness before attacking. While pups were usually just playing with each other, he wasn't so sure about the women.

He hadn't had a chance to ask Kitty about her conversation with Serena. Kitty had been too eager to ask her own questions and keep him busy.

"I love your yellow diamond belly ring," Serena said. "It dazzles."

"Thank you," Kitty purred. "It's a gift from Jared. I believe he found it in Holland."

"Oh." Serena darted a glare at him that could've melted ice cubes.

Jared was definitely not going to start the grill until he knew they'd be cooking something other than him.

"Jared does have surprisingly good taste when it comes to jewelry," Serena added.

Jared groaned and swallowed hard. Surely Serena wasn't going to lift her short skirt to show off the pussy ring he'd bought her. He grimaced when she slid a hand down her thigh. She gave

223

him a mocking grin.

"He's also demonstrated decent taste in women," Serena arched an eyebrow at Kitty, "on occasion."

Kitty laughed. Jared gave her credit for not rising to Serena's bait. Maybe Kitty wasn't looking for a fight after all. Seth gave him a questioning look and he shrugged in response. He wasn't about to get between the women at this point.

"Speaking of Jared's taste," Kitty said, "I'm thinking a little appetizer might be in order before we start cooking. Maybe we can clear away some tension at the same time."

Unsmiling, Kitty stepped across to where he was standing. She locked her gaze on his, undid the snap on his shorts, and pulled down on its zipper.

"What are you doing?" he groaned as she slid down to her knees.

"What does it look like? I'm sampling a delicious appetizer."

Jared wet his lips and closed his eyes briefly as Kitty went down on him. Obviously delighting in putting on a show, she was in no hurry. He stared at Serena and Seth, who stood as if rooted in cement watching his houseguest claim her appetizer. Serena looked like she was about to explode.

Kitty rocked back on the balls of her feet and dropped him from her mouth. The sudden rush of cool air was chilling. She used both hands to stroke him. She kissed the tip of his cock. He saw her turn and beckon to Serena.

"You better get down here and share this guy. I think he's missed you as much as you've missed him."

Serena smiled broadly and dropped to her knees, murmuring, "Thanks."

Kitty stood and kissed him full on the lips. He tasted his own muskiness when she broke away. She smiled. "I believe you're in a warm place, and I've got another appetizer to try out."

Serena took him deep into her throat and he tried to keep track of Kitty, who quickly helped Seth dispense of his shorts. He watched her plant kisses along Seth's length.

"I never did get a good look at this fellow the other day," Kitty teased. "Well, at least not good enough." She cupped Seth's balls and Jared watched his friend rise on his toes as Kitty took his cock deep in her mouth.

"Jesus," Jared groaned as both women bobbed up and down. Kitty had been playing with all of them. Certainly she'd decided to share him with Serena before they ever came out onto the patio. Vaguely, he wondered how that boded for their future.

The surge started in his balls. Jared clamped down and pulled away from Serena. She looked at him in surprise. "I want to sample an appetizer too."

"Oh, of course." Serena rose to her feet and

kissed his lips where Kitty's scent still remained. "It's good to be with you again. She's a good woman, Jared."

"I've noticed," he replied, spreading several blankets on the patio. When he was ready, he motioned for Serena. Smiling, she stretched out on the blanket, spread her legs and then spread her pussy lips. "Is this the appetizer you're wanting?"

"It is," he said, stretching out between her legs.

She held her vulva open between thumb and forefinger. "Come and get it," Serena said, grinning, "pussy is served."

Jared didn't hesitate. He dipped his tongue in the center of Serena's pinkness. She was already creaming, and he'd bet neither of them had patience for any more teasing. He'd missed her. He really had.

"So good," Serena cooed, pulling on his ears. "Yes, deeper. Tongue fuck me."

Jared probed as deep as he could. For Serena, he knew exactly which buttons to push and he proceeded to push them. Her squeals were joined by those of Kitty's.

He caught a glimpse of Seth eating Kitty only a couple feet away from where he and Serena lay. So they had followed his lead. He heard Kitty wail, "Glorious. You're going to make me come."

Jared chuckled and curled his tongue higher into Serena.

"That's it," she hollered. She bucked against his tongue as he knew she would. She shifted slightly.

He held his tongue in place, letting her grind against it until she crashed. "Holy shit!" she screamed, "I'm lost."

"Drink me, drink me," Kitty pleaded with Seth.

Jared had no doubt Seth was complying with Kitty's request as she mewed small sounds of pleasure. He rested his head on Serena's belly and felt her continuing to nurse aftershocks.

Jared sucked air into his lungs and opened his eyes to see Seth smiling triumphantly at him as he too caught his breath waiting for Kitty. His vision in yellow had certainly arranged for very appealing appetizers for all of them.

His eyes widened when he noticed that sometime, probably during the throes of orgasm, the women had joined hands. Their fingers remained intertwined between them as each in her own way embraced this post climactic glow.

Jared closed his eyes and smiled. Each woman posed a formidable powerhouse to handle alone. If they joined forces, did he and Seth stand a chance of surviving?

- o -

Much later, Kitty sat curled in one of Jared's living room chairs and watched the three lovers on the carpet. The three of them seemed to know intuitively what a partner might want or desire. Perhaps that was a benefit of being long term lovers.

Serena lay astride Jared gliding slowly back and forth, stroking Jared's massive cock with her vagina. At the same time she sucked on her husband's penis as he knelt beside her.

Kitty shuddered. She knew very well what Serena was experiencing because she'd been in that same position a little earlier in the evening. Thank goodness they'd all agreed on not actually cooking a big meal. They'd done quite fine snacking on cheeses, cold cuts, and each other.

She hadn't expected sharing to be this much fun. She enjoyed watching nearly as much as not—nearly. And it wasn't exactly like the observer was left out. Kitty unfolded her legs to begin lightly tracing the sides of her vulva without taking her gaze off the entwined lovers.

Seth pulled away from his wife's mouth and stood. He glanced at Kitty while reaching for a condom. "Like you," he said, "Serena is quite partial to man sandwiches."

She nodded and wet her lips and watched intently as Seth positioned himself between Jared's legs to nuzzle his wife's bottom. Kitty glanced back at Jared. Her mouth fell ajar. He was staring at Serena with that same kind of brilliance that he sometimes did with her. Serena nibbled on his lips and Jared preened like a man in love.

Kitty's mouth went dry. Her hand stilled on her pussy. She'd seen that look before on Jared. She just hadn't interpreted it as a look of love before. Damn, she was in trouble. She'd responded to that look just like Serena was. Kitty shivered. But she didn't love Jared. Serena probably did, but *she* didn't.

Serena stopped and winked at her before saying, "Anytime you're ready. Looks like someone is enjoying the show."

Kitty stopped breathing as Seth pushed his cock into Serena's ass. Kitty mimicked his movement, shoving her hand lower until she could widen her own asshole with an index finger.

"That's right, girl," Serena said to her, "join us. Oh my..."

Kitty nodded as Seth completed the sandwich by sinking all the way into his wife's ass. Kitty groaned as her finger slipped in past her knuckle until it could go no farther.

"I could've done that for you," Jared grunted, slowly thrusting into Serena.

"Too late," Kitty managed to say. "Another time. Focus on Serena."

He nodded and dragged Serena's mouth down to his. They exchanged tongues as Seth and Jared began pummeling Serena alternately with one cock in her ass and one in her pussy. Serena's eyes rolled back. She pulled away from Jared's mouth and roared, "Fuck me!"

Serena was right when she'd said hearing flesh pound flesh intensified the experience of watching. Kitty drove her finger in and out of her ass, keeping time with Seth. She sniffed the air, unable to separate the intermingled scents of perspiration and pleasure. She couldn't determine if they were each in their own little erotic world or if their souls had merged. All she knew was she was about to have a glorious climax. She dropped her free hand to her clit.

"I'm coming, guys," Serena wailed.

Kitty's legs stiffened and her heartbeat raced as she furiously worked on her ass and clit.

"That's it!" Serena yelled. "Don't hold back."

"Impossible," Seth groaned, bucking into his wife.

Kitty smiled when she saw Jared's hips jerking and heard his familiar *son of a bitch*. Did he know he said that nearly every time he climaxed?

Kitty lurched forward into a pretzel. She'd been nurturing her orgasm, but this was going to be powerful. She didn't stop pushing herself to the edge until she leaped into the abyss. Gingerly she withdrew her finger, but she remained in place, sitting on the chair with her head between her knees, gulping for air.

She squeezed her eyes against the pain and the pleasure. Visions of red vied with those of black. Jared's look of adoration flashed before her. She swallowed. She tried to find feeling in her toes, but couldn't.

She had no idea how long she remained like that, seemingly partially paralyzed, before she felt familiar strong hands massaging her neck.

"You okay?"

Jared's voice helped bring her back. "I will be,"

she mumbled. "That does feel good."

At some point, she felt comfortable enough to open her eyes. Jared stood next to her, continuing to draw small concentric circles on her shoulders with his finger pads. Serena sat on her husband's lap nuzzling his chin.

When Serena noticed her watching, she said, "Watching can be a turn on too, right?"

Kitty nodded her head and straightened to a sitting position. "I wasn't prepared for how much of a turn on it could be."

She looked sheepishly at Jared. "I'm done. I hope no one minds, maybe it's my age, but I've got to get some sleep."

"We'll be leaving," Serena said, standing and looking around for her clothes. "I have to drive in and pick up Savannah before noon tomorrow."

Kitty didn't have the strength to get up as she watched Serena and Seth dress. Once dressed, Serena gave her an odd look before coming over to her.

"This was fantastic. I hope you enjoyed yourself." Serena bent down and kissed her cheek. "Can we do this again sometime?"

Kitty gave the redhead a half smile. "Spectacular. I hope we can."

"If we put our minds together, I'm sure will come up with more opportunities. Good night, guys."

Serena kissed Jared good night and Seth leaned down to kiss her good night.

Once the door closed behind them, Jared pulled her up into his arms and lifted her off her feet. "We need to get you to bed," he said, carrying her toward the stairs.

She yawned in his arms. "Thanks. I don't know if I've ever felt older. Those two could've carried on all night."

Jared chuckled. "From what I saw, I don't think either one of us is ready for rockers at the old folks home. But maybe a decade does make some difference."

Kitty leaned away from him. "You mean she isn't even thirty?"

"Not quite. Don't worry about it. We're all getting older day by day."

"And tomorrow we'll be another day older."

"That's right. We just have to decide how we're going to live each day."

Kitty drifted, not wanting to deal with tomorrow until she absolutely had to.

- o -

Jared awoke with a start. He glanced around in the early morning darkness, unable to determine what had awakened him. He cast his arm out to caress Kitty.

He jerked to a sitting position. Not only wasn't she there, the sheets were cold. "What the hell," he mumbled, swinging his legs over the side of the bed.

He headed for the bathroom. Re-entering the bedroom, he yawned, grabbed a robe and headed downstairs. He'd thought Kitty would sleep for a week after last night. Maybe she had a craving for coffee or something.

When he reached the end of the hall way, he frowned. There was no light on in the kitchen. Hurriedly, he looked room to room. He called out her name. He slid the patio door open and stepped outside. The early morning chill slapped his face like aftershave. She wasn't in the pool. Kitty had disappeared.

His shoulders sagging, Jared turned and made his way back to the bedroom. As if sleepwalking, he put on some clothes. He'd check the stable, though that didn't seem like a place she'd go to.

He stepped out the front door and looked around. Nothing. "Damn," he muttered. He turned and raced back to the bedroom. Why hadn't he thought about checking for her luggage earlier?

He yanked the closet doors open. "Son of a bitch!" He'd thought she had more spine than this. She'd left him. That was obvious. She hadn't even bothered leaving a note.

- o -

Kitty popped another chocolate covered cherry in her mouth. She winced. She might as well be eating sawdust. Nothing tasted right anymore, not even her favorite depression treat.

And she didn't need a shrink to tell her she was depressed. She'd earned it. Nearly a week had passed since she'd sneaked out of the adobe ranch house in the wee early morning hours to meet the cab she'd called after Jared had fallen asleep. No, she hadn't sneaked off. That was too grand. She'd slunk off, as if she were the most cowardly beast on earth.

She'd panicked, pure and simple. She hadn't been able to shake the image of love on Jared's face for Serena, but worse, for her. That look still haunted her. But her own cowardly actions haunted her even more.

She'd never had a man look at her like that before, so maybe she should forgive herself for not at first recognizing it for what it was. Jared had fallen in love with her. That he also loved Serena didn't trouble her at all. What troubled her was…

She popped another chocolate covered cherry in her mouth and looked frantically around her kitchen. She couldn't get away from him. They'd made love in every room of the house. She brushed her fingers over the end of the kitchen table where she'd lain while Jared had leisurely eaten her pussy as a midnight snack.

She shook her head, trying to focus clearly. She resisted the urge to ease the tension in her throbbing pussy. She pressed her palms against the table top. What troubled her most was, she couldn't explain her own feelings.

She missed the damn guy. She'd always been able to move on quickly to another lover. She never allowed herself to look in the rearview mirror.

She missed seeing his mustache curl as he smiled. His soft drawl when he wanted to cajole. His snapping eyes when she taunted him. His being so completely at ease when he played with Savannah. His pride for his horses. His capacity for dreaming for the future. His apparent effort to satisfy her in every way possible.

Kitty bit into another cherry and set it aside half eaten. She shivered and hugged herself. Jared had even provided her with a second cock. She licked her lips. What else would she ever want?

Even watching the men with Serena was enormously provocative and satisfying. What did Serena make of her abrupt departure? Had Serena ever experienced the kind of fear that threatened to consume?

Kitty remembered the love so evidently portrayed on Serena's face encouraging her men to love her. A wave of jealousy swept through her. Kitty slumped at the kitchen table trying not to shake. Her efforts proved useless. She quaked and sobbed.

She pressed her forehead against the tabletop, letting her body have its way. She drifted, trying to find the next breath. Images floated behind her closed eyelids.

You don't deserve to be loved. It was the voice of

her father.

"You're wrong, Daddy. I do deserve to be loved. And I want to love."

She blotted out the picture of her enraged father. The image of two couples making love on Jared's living room carpet came into focus. She grinned and sighed. More images came into view: images of hurriedly claiming each other that first time in her entryway; images of riding Jared on the western saddle; images of watching them in his bedroom mirrors as he took her ass after giving her a thorough spanking.

Kitty jerked up abruptly and dug her fists into her eyes. Could it be? As she'd replayed that scene she'd watched in the mirrors, she saw the same kind of adoration and love reflected on *her* face as she'd seen on his and on Serena's.

"Holy shit," she murmured. Her nipples strained hard against her robe.

Standing, she ignored everything but her dilemma. This was not a time to be sidetracked.

She'd blown it badly. She paced, gulping in air, wishing she could turn back the clock. Had Jared already moved on? He hadn't reached out to her, but she'd hardly expected him to. He wouldn't beg.

She wasn't into groveling either, but if what she was feeling really was real, she'd better figure out some way to regain his attention. She knew far too well that opportunities for real love were rare.

Kitty felt her body hum as she switched gears

from berating herself to devising a plan to make things right with Jared. She couldn't risk simply showing up on his doorstep again. Having him slam the door in her face could be too devastating — even for her.

Kitty stopped pacing. He'd caught her attention initially by sending her roses, and then they'd gone through a gift exchange that culminated in his coming to Chicago.

She inhaled deeply. It was worth a try. She'd find a gift he couldn't ignore.

- o -

Looking at his travel schedule for the following week, Jared tried to feel some excitement. He always enjoyed Zurich. Maybe what he needed was an understanding Swiss woman. He could always tack on an extra week and fly to Amsterdam. He grimaced. Would Maya be particularly understanding? She'd probably demand to know why he was sitting on his hands if he'd finally found the woman he wanted to spend his life with. She'd question his pride.

"Pride," Jared grunted. This wasn't about pride. Kitty had slithered off into the dark to escape him. That was that. He wouldn't chase of after her — no matter what Maya thought or even what Serena thought.

He glanced toward his open office door. Serena had been staring darts at him ever since Kitty left, as if it was his fault or somehow within his power to make things right again for all of them.

He did not have a magic wand. There had been no word at all from Kitty explaining her actions, apologizing, or anything else.

Jared stood. He was so damn tired of replaying every word the two of them had ever exchanged. He needed to move on and put her behind him. Hopefully, his European trip would help. Right now the best thing to do was ignore his feelings and everyone else. He'd go saddle up his favorite mare and head out across the range. That might prove good for what ailed him.

He stepped into the outer office and quickly realized escape wasn't going to be that easy. Serena stood at one of the file cabinets rifling through papers. Instead of wearing her usual pullover and jeans, she had on a short skirt and a blouse open nearly to her navel.

Jared glared at his personal assistant, who likely believed she knew how to cure him of his blues.

"She's been gone over a week, Jared. Don't you think it's about time for you to stop moping around here like a lost puppy?" The redhead came to stand before him. She held his gaze steady as she undid the top two buttons of his shirt.

"I can help," she murmured. "You know I can. Seth and I are both worried for you." She reached between them to encourage his semi-hard cock.

He shook his head and took a step back.

"Don't," he said, grasping her wrists.

"Why?"

Serena's pain cut through him.

"Why are you rejecting me—me and Seth? We were happy before she came here. We can be happy again. Can't we?"

Jared tried not to respond to his long-time lover, now sticking her tongue out at him. Reluctantly he pulled her into his arms and buried his nose in her hair. She hugged him tight. He grabbed her butt to keep her from grinding against his crotch.

"Don't," he whispered. "I'm not rejecting you and Seth. I never will. You must know that. I'm just not ready yet." He lifted her skirt with one hand and popped her bare bottom with the other.

She jerked back in surprise.

"Now," he said, lifting her chin and brushing his lips across hers. "Be a patient girl. I'll come around. Probably by the time I get back from Europe I'll have her out of my system."

"Maybe you should be going to Chicago instead of Europe," Serena snapped. "I've never seen you like this before. Kitty marked you good."

Serena turned back to her desk and Jared headed for the exit, but she had one more parting shot. "On second thought, I don't want you fucking me until you're straight with Kitty—one way or another." She scowled. "And I doubt dashing off to Europe will resolve anything."

Two hours later Jared stalked toward his office. His ride had cleared his mind some and he was about to straighten out his assistant who was so determined to be the guardian of his heart. He'd toyed with the idea of laying her across her desk and proving her very wrong about not wanting to fuck him, but then that might be what she wanted. Even though he'd known Serena much longer than he'd known Kitty, he didn't think either woman was transparent when they wanted to remain mysterious.

Instead, he'd tell Serena to butt out. He knew what it'd take to put Kitty behind him. The European trip was the medicine he needed. Maybe he wouldn't stop over in Amsterdam. The twin blondes he'd known in Brussels might be a better option. They'd be happy to see him and wouldn't be at all interested in prying into his personal life. In that regard, they'd be much more reliable than Maya.

He slammed the office door loudly behind him. Serena didn't flinch. She gave him a broad smile, as if she hadn't just bitched at him a couple hours earlier, and pointed toward his open office doorway.

"Before you try chewing on me," she said, batting an eyelash, "you may want to check out your mail. I left it on your desk."

"Don't go anywhere," he groused. "I still owe you a piece of my mind."

She shrugged. "I don't care, though I'd rather

240

have you chewing me out. Maybe you'll think differently in a few minutes."

Jared stalked past his desk and on into his office, slamming that door behind him. He'd had about enough of her—of all women, for that matter.

He scowled down at the package on his desk. Immediately he recognized the handwriting and the address.

He sighed and slouched down in his desk chair. Should he open it? Was this a parting gift? He shook his head and glanced quickly at the door. How long would Serena wait before barging in?

Cautiously, he opened the package—*A Pictorial Guide to the Kama Sutra*. "What the hell?"

There was no card. He opened the book cover and read the inscription.

Hi sunshine man,

Sorry for my abrupt departure, but I needed space and time. As you can see, I've been doing some profound reading of late. Looks like we may have unfinished business. We didn't get around to half the possibilities described here.

Is it too late for more adventures?
KP

Jared flipped through the pages of intertwined lovers. He smiled at several pictures thinking how easily he and Kitty could have been the photographer's subjects. He eyed others closely, realizing Kitty was right. They hadn't nearly explored all the possibilities.

Unfinished business. He tapped his finger on the book. So Kitty was willing to take another step or two with him. He sniffed the air, trying to inhale her scent that must cling to the book. Would she really want more adventure when she discovered the stakes? This time he'd settle for no less than all of her—body and soul. He'd accept no less, because she already had his.

He started to get up to tell Serena to cancel his European trip when she entered his office without knocking. He grinned. Shouldn't he be more annoyed with his assistant for intruding?

Serena flashed a broad smile. "Looks like you're coming back to life. So what did she send this time?"

Jared shoved the book toward her.

Serena flipped through the pages. "This seems rather straghtforward." She giggled and pointed at a page. "And look at this, a woman with two guys. Kitty is sending a message loud and clear."

"Check out the next page. Two women and a guy." Jared smirked at Serena's scrunched features.

"I'm sure she didn't want to deface the book by ripping out a page." She leveled a glare at him. "So what's next? The ball appears to be in your court."

He shrugged, but she wasn't having anything to do with his feigned nonchalance. "I haven't decided yet. But when I do, everything will be on the line. I won't settle for less than marriage."

Serena chuckled and leaned across the desk to kiss his forehead. "That sounds more like our Jared. Do you want me to cancel your European reservations?"

He shook his head. "I'll let you know."

"I've already routed them through Chicago— just in case."

He straightened. "I'm not flying direct?"

She withdrew slightly. "I just said I have you connecting in Chicago."

"Great. Are all women as conniving as you and Kitty?"

"You," she said, looking demure, "probably have experience with more women than I do."

"Don't try looking so innocent. It doesn't become you." Jared tapped his fingers on his desk. "And if I can convince her to marry me, that doesn't mean Kitty will want a repeat performance like we had in my living room."

"I'm not worried." Serena drew herself up on her toes. "Maybe I know Kitty better than you do in some ways. If she agrees to marry you, it'll probably be on the condition that she still has access to two cocks. She strikes me as a woman as fond of two cocks as I am. And," she wet her lips, "she and I have an agreement. If I share Seth's cock with her, I get to share my pussy with you. That's a bargain you can count on, lover. Don't assume otherwise. You won't be able to keep her

243

entirely to yourself."

"That's fair, I suppose, because I'll never give you up entirely."

Serena smirked. "I know that," she said softly. "All kidding aside, so does Kitty. She wouldn't be sending you that book if she thought otherwise."

He nodded and glanced back down at the book, open to the picture of a woman sandwiched between two guys. He didn't doubt Serena's assessment of Kitty. Kitty had nearly said the same thing when they were together in Chicago. Wasn't that why he'd introduced her to Seth?

He glanced back up at Serena. "Why don't you go do something useful? I've got some serious thinking to do." He scrunched his mouth. "I'll let you know about the reservations when I've made up my mind."

"Okay boss," Serena quipped. "Just don't take too much time. We don't know how long Kitty will wait."

CHAPTER THIRTEEN

Two days later, Kitty stared in disbelief at the contents of the package that had arrived at her house. There was no card. The return address was Jared's.

She tried to steady her breathing as she flipped through the real estate guide for Jared's region in the San Diego foothills. She felt her eyes widen as she saw some of the prices. She'd thought she was quite jaded by high real estate prices, but the possible commissions on those California properties boggled her mind. No doubt that was Jared's plan.

She set the guide aside and gingerly lifted the blue and white garter, as if it might burn. She brought it to her nose slowly and sniffed it. Jared didn't have to enclose a card. His intentions were obvious — blue and white garters were for brides. She'd never had the chance to wear one.

Kitty fought the urge to get up and flee from her house. Where would she run? She wanted to explore more possibilities with him — and with Serena and Seth — but he wasn't accepting that. He wanted it all. She'd thought about those next steps, but not about taking them now.

She'd have to respond, but how? She couldn't ignore the feeling of being cornered. Should she pick up the phone and clarify what she wanted? That assumed she knew what she wanted.

Would he call her?

Should she fly to San Diego? Was he already on a plane to Chicago?

What would she do if he rang the doorbell right now? She swallowed hard. She knew what she'd *do*. She'd hug him fiercely and drag him upstairs to her bed, if they could make it out of the entryway.

But she had no clue what to *say* to him.

The following morning, Kitty skipped breakfast and drove to the track, where Rebecca had agreed to meet her for coffee. The woman hadn't hesitated to join her, and Kitty had surprised herself when she realized how soothing the track had become for her.

She glanced up from her coffee to see Rebecca staring at her with a twinkle and a twinge of sadness. Kitty no longer felt particularly soothed.

"So you finally found your man?" Rebecca traced the rim of the coffee mug. "I'm pleased for you. Why don't you look more pleased?"

"I didn't say Jared was my man," she huffed, feeling her cheeks warm.

"You didn't have to say it in so many words. It shows. Lawrence will be happy for you, too."

"I didn't say I was going to marry the guy." Exasperated, Kitty rapped her fingers on the table and gulped her coffee. She set the cup back down and couldn't avoid the tremble in her fingers. "You've been married twice."

"And happily both times, and I still owe you for introducing me to Lawrence."

"How did you know?" Kitty hesitated and inhaled. "How did you know you were making the right decision to marry?"

"Ah. I never thought I'd see the day that confident Kitty Paige might get cold feet." Rebecca chuckled. "It's perfectly normal. I did with both my husbands."

"You did?"

"Uh, huh. Marriage is a risky business."

"I agree with that."

Rebecca raised her palm. "Let me finish. Marrying was a risk. I'll never deny that. I weighed my feelings and his. I tried to imagine our lives together." She cocked her head to the side. "It wasn't difficult to imagine my life *without* marrying."

Kitty winced. "I suppose not."

"You see," Rebecca continued, "your decision has risks both ways. It may be risky leaping into marriage, but not doing so carries its own risks. Those risks may be more comfortable because you have a better understanding of what they are. The risk of marrying in that sense is for the more adventurous among us, I suppose."

Kitty glared at Rebecca — suddenly she sounded smug. "And you were willing to risk twice."

"That's right. And I don't regret either risk. So

247

what's holding you back? You don't want to lose some of your freedom? You prefer living alone, taking a man when you want one? Afraid of the unknown? Not sure enough about Jared or yourself to take the chance?"

Kitty looked wildly around the small room. The walls were coming in on her. She shook her head. She didn't have the answers to all of those questions — maybe to none of them.

"I'm sorry, Kitty. I didn't mean to push you."

"No," Kitty stammered, "I asked. I wanted to hear what you had to say. Don't apologize." Kitty reached for the tab. "But I do have to be going. You've given me much to think about." She stared at Rebecca through blurry eyes. "Thank you. I have to be alone."

Her heart still clutched when she got in her car. Was he worth the risk? She had so much to lose. She started the engine and revved up the car. But Rebecca was right — if she let Jared walk out of her life, she had a lot to lose, too. Too much.

How much time would he give her? She thought of the blue and white garter and wiped tears from her eyes. Damn him for pushing her so fast. Damn her for being so entrenched.

Kitty dashed to the ringing phone as soon as she opened the door to her house. She glanced quickly at the caller I.D. as she reached for the phone. She gulped. He wasn't going to give her long at all.

Without further thought she brought the phone to her ear. "Hello."

"Hi, Kitty. Good to hear your voice."

He sounded so reserved, so business-like. "It's good to hear yours, too. I don't know where to begin."

"I cancelled a trip to Europe."

"Oh." She frowned. Wasn't he going to let her apologize?

"I'm coming to Chicago instead."

"Oh." Why couldn't she say more than *oh?* She must sound totally stupid.

"I'm coming to get you, Kitty."

His raspy voice sent a shiver racing up her spine. "I know."

"I probably can't get there until tomorrow noon. You'll be at home."

Was that a question or a command? She wet her lips. "I'll be here. I'll be waiting for you."

"Good."

Kitty stared at the phone when she heard him hang up.

"Oh my God," she mumbled, flopping down in a kitchen chair. He was coming to get her. There was no mistake about what he meant. He was coming to claim her as his wife. And she hadn't told him to stay away. She'd told him she'd be waiting for him.

When had she reached her decision? When she'd gotten up to leave Rebecca at the track café? On the drive back to her house? When she'd heard

Jared's voice on the phone? When he'd told her he was coming for her?

It didn't matter. She stood and wiped at her eyes. She sighed and then began to laugh. He was coming for her. Her cowboy was riding in from the west to claim his bride.

She hadn't told him not to come, but how could he be so sure? But he'd probably been certain about them much longer than she had.

Tomorrow noon. Good God. Why hadn't she asked more questions, or even said yes, she wanted to marry him? Now she'd have to wait until tomorrow. How many times would she second guess herself? Too bad she couldn't simply sleep till then.

Kitty tried not to look at the clock on the fireplace mantel. That didn't seem to make the time go by any faster. She smoothed out her long plaid skirt. She'd chosen it purposefully, not wanting to seem overly eager in case she'd misunderstood him—though she didn't think she had. The slit halfway up her thigh should prove provocative enough. And the off-the-shoulder smocked top hardly made her look matronly.

She crossed her legs at her ankles and grinned, looking at her high heel sandals. Jared was a softie when it came to high heels. She'd learned that about him the very first night they'd met at Susan's wedding reception.

She lay back against the couch. So much had

happened since that weekend. Had Jared talked at all to Jackson about her? She'd love to have listened in on *that* conversation.

She started when she heard a car pull into the driveway. She stood and peeked out the window to see Jared paying a cab driver. So that answered one question. He didn't expect to need a rental car for a quick exit.

She waited for him to ring the doorbell before opening the door. He strolled into the entryway and set down his travel bag.

She watched him rake his gaze up and down her. If he was disappointed she wore a long skirt, he didn't show it. "Hi," she said softly. "Welcome back." She held out her arms and he took her into his.

She laced her arms around his neck and pulled his mouth down to hers. His lips crushed against hers. She had difficulty breathing, and from the sound of Jared, he wasn't any more calm than she was.

She stepped away from him, holding his hand. "Come on. You must be starved. I've made us a light lunch."

"Starved," he said, beaming at her. "Starved for you."

She shook her head. "Not right away. Let's not act like a couple wild animals."

"It wouldn't be the first time," he groused, squeezing her fingers but following her lead.

"I'm quite aware of that.".

251

When they got to the kitchen, she directed Jared to a chair, which he took reluctantly. She set about pouring coffee for both of them and put out a plate of fruits, cheeses, and sliced sausage.

"Eat," she ordered, pulling up a chair for herself.

He nibbled on an orange slice. "I'm much more interested in hearing what you have to say than eating."

"We'll see about that." She smirked and curled her fingers around his. "So you came to get me."

"That's what I said," he drawled.

"No lasso, no chains."

"They're in my overnight bag."

"I see." She leaned back, inhaled deeply and let it out slowly. "What do you really have in mind, Jared? Hauling me off to your dungeon? Setting me up as your mistress? Tell me."

"You know the answer to that. I want you to be my wife."

"It's hard for a girl to know unless the guy says what he means. So are you proposing to me?"

Amusement flickered across his eyes. "You know I am, Kitty. I didn't know you could be so coy."

"No one has ever proposed to me. I'm not sure I'd recognize the words."

"Ah." He tipped back his head and chuckled. His smile broadened as he moved off the chair to kneel before her on one knee. "So, Kitty, will you marry me?"

Kitty was surprised by her own clear headedness. She smiled at Jared. "You want me to move to your ranch?"

He nodded. "If you would. I'd be willing to try to live both there and here, if you want."

"No, that won't be necessary. I've lived here my whole life and spent most of that time working. California might be a nice change of pace. And as you made clear, they do sell houses there, too. I will want my own office at the ranch."

His smile broadened. "So you're saying *yes?*"

"Serena and Seth?" She tilted her head to the side.

Jared frowned and exhaled. "I won't give up Serena entirely. I can't."

"Good." Kitty's heart fluttered. "Then I get to share Seth from time to time."

"Serena and Seth are counting on that. So are you going to say yes, or are you going to make me grow old and gray kneeling before you? Oh!" he exclaimed. "How could I forget?"

Kitty watched him dig into his trousers and produce a small box. She could feel her eyes widen. This was no longer abstract, if it ever had been.

Jared opened the box and plucked out a sizeable diamond flanked by two smaller diamonds. He took her left hand and, apparently seeing no resistance in her smile, pushed the ring part way onto her finger. "So do you have an answer?"

She nodded and drew his other hand along the slit of her long skirt until she curled his fingers around the blue and white garter hugging her thigh. Her skirt fell away, revealing what he was holding onto.

He glanced down and looked back at her with surprise. "You knew all along," he challenged.

"Of course I did," she said softly, pushing her finger forward until the ring passed over her knuckle. "Yes, I'll marry you, and I had hoped we wouldn't have any problems with our understandings about living space and Serena and Seth."

He rose and kissed her soundly.

She curled her hand around his wrist and stood. "Let me clear the table," she said.

"But now…"

She shook her head at him as she wiped the table. She tossed the rag toward the sink. "But now," she said, sliding up onto the table, "I'm ready to serve my starving man."

She hiked her skirt up over her waist and slid back on the table until her high heels rested on the table top. The precious look on Jared's face would've assuaged any doubts she might still harbor about marrying him, but she had none.

He wet his lips and grazed her thigh with his fingers. "That garter looks terrific on you. It helps set off a bare pussy extremely well."

She chuckled. "Maybe we'll want to buy me a garter belt and stockings for a wedding present."

"You can count on that."

"But this will have to do for now," she added, spreading her labia just enough to draw his attention.

He flicked his tongue out at her and lowered his head.

She moaned when his tongue slid along her separated folds. "Oh damn," she squealed. "Maybe we should've done this first."

Kitty locked her legs around his back and interlaced her fingers in his hair. "Don't rush, but I think when you're done with lunch, I'll have a hunger to fill also."

He rose up to face her. "I was hoping you might. So I guess you're not a girl who has to wait until her wedding night."

She burst into laughter and pushed his head back down to her throbbing loins. "Be a good boy. I've never spanked a fiancée, but I'm willing to try." His lips covered her clit and she lurched forward.

Keeping his mouth in place, Jared winked up at her. "And I love a woman who keeps her promises."

"I do," Kitty, lolling her head from side to side. "And I will. Oh hell, I'm coming." She squeezed his head between her thighs. "Wait for me."

His words came to her from a distance. "I will always wait for you."

The End

About the Author

Adriana Kraft is the pen name for a husband/wife team writing *Erotic Romance for Two, Three or More.* The award-winning pair has published over thirty erotic romance novels and novellas to outstanding reviews. Long and Short Reviews: *"scorching hot…refreshing...something to read when you want straight up hotness."* Romance Junkies: *"filled with warmth, blazing hot sex, well-developed characters…not for the faint of heart."* Romantic pairings include straight m/f, lesbian, bisexual, ménage and polyamory, in both contemporary and paranormal settings.

We hope you enjoyed *The Best Man,* and we love hearing from readers! You can find all our links at our website:

http://adrianakraft.com

More Books from Adriana Kraft

Smoldering Passion
Passion Series: Book One
Center Director Harry Gage hires Melissa Hopkins to have sex on camera. When smoldering lust and desire ignite into burning passion, is it love or just sex?

Five Stars: "Exploring the complexities of sex, romance, age differences, power positions…a great ending." Billie D, Amazon

Anticipation
winging Games Series: Book One
To spice up their relationship, Brett and Jennifer have just entered the swinging world - will their next encounter live up to their fantasies?

"This story is hot … imagination takes on a life of its own." Examiner.com

Seducing Cat
Meghan's Playhouse: Book One
What could college English professor Caitlin Shanahan ever have in common with the brash carpenter Kurt Davis? Meghan Keenan, that's what. The twenty year old sprite decides to bring the unlikely pair together through sharing her sexual delights with each of them. Town-gown relationships have never been better…

Four and a half Kisses: "Left me waiting and wanting to read more…" Joni, Two Lips Reviews

Colors of the Night
Aria: Book One
A love triangle with a dazzling immortal goddess – will it ignite or extinguish the dying embers of a contemporary couple's love?

Top Pick "This book is excellent. I love the idea of the Goddess of Love…" MonicaBBB, Night Owl Reviews

Coming soon:

Cassie's Hope
Riders Up! Book One

What happens when a fiercely loyal widowed half-Ute cowboy meets a fiery redhead with an Irish temper to match? Cassidy O'Hanlon – Cassie, to her friends – has set aside her Chicago career for six months to train racehorses for her dad after his stroke.

Furious the interloper has shipped in a ringer from the Chicago circuit to his Wyoming turf, Rancher/trainer Clint Travers sets out to put her in her place. Sparks fly immediately, but after their rocky start, the two quickly forge a passionate relationship, and he follows her to Chicago.

When it becomes clear someone is drugging Cassie's horse, Clint sets out to solve the mystery, but storms off in a cloud of wounded pride when suspicions turn to him.

Can love trump pride?

Cassie's Hope will be released in October, 2013. Watch our blog for release information, buy links, and a chance to obtain *Cassie's Hope* free at Amazon.

Chapter One of *Cassie's Hope* won fourth place and a marvelous cover by Judy Bullard in the Romance Junkies 2012 Writing Contest. You can read the chapter at this link:

http://www.contestjunkies.com/artman/publish/Cassie_s_Hope.php